Sweet Tea and Afternoon Tales

More Stories from the South

Sweet Tea and Afternoon Tales

More Stories from the South

Gulf Coast Writers Association

Edited by
Philip L. Levin and Dixon Hearne

AWOC.COM Publishing
Denton, Texas

The following stories have appeared previously in print or online. Permission to reprint is granted by the authors, who are the rightful holders of copyright:

"Southern Charms" (excerpt), *Oxford So and So*, July-August 2007, by permission of Marilyn Allgood.

"Original Sin, the Seven Deadlines Come Home to Roost," *The Paper Journey Press*, by permission of Shannon Rulè Bardwell.

"Magnolia Veil," *Brick Street Press Anthology*, 2009, by permission of Lucy J. Dixon.

"Voodoo Bayou," *Kansas City Voices Magazine*, 2008, by permission of Fred Farris.

"Appearances," *Amazon Shorts*, July 2006, by permission of John M. Floyd.

"Let Me Down Easy," *Motif: Writing by Ear: An Anthology of Writings About Music*, by permission of Denton Loving.

"Motorcycle Mama," *Magnolia Quarterly*, by permission of Philip L. Levin.

"Redemption at Station Creek," *Kudzu*, 2008, by permission of Sylvia Lynch.

"Goose Chase," *Oasis Journal*, 2008, by permission of Jan Rider.

"Truth and Mercy," *World Wide Writers Anthology*, Amazon Shorts, by permission of Richelle Putnam.

"Swee' Daddy's Big Sanyo," *Moonshine Review*, June 2008, by permission of Bob Strother.

"The Break In," *Humor Press* web site, (appears here in slightly different version) by permission of Glanda Widger.

Cover Art: Alice Moseley

Published by AWOC.COM Publishing, P.O. Box 2819, Denton, TX 76202, USA. No part of this publication may be reproduced, stored in a retrieval system, or transmitted in any form or by any means, electronic, mechanical, recording, or otherwise, without the prior written permission of the author(s).

Manufactured in the United States of America

ISBN: 978-0-037660-56-0

Table of Contents

Acknowledgements

The authors wish to thank all the writers who answered our Call for Submissions. We contacted sixty-four writers groups across the country, many of whom included our announcement in their newsletters and at their websites. We salute these fellow writers for their interest and generosity.

Very special thanks to Victoria Olsen for her assistance with website announcements, editorial review and advice again this year.

We also wish to thank Tim Moseley for allowing us to use his mother, Alice Moseley's painting, "Barbecue, Picture Hats and Cool Mint Juleps," for our cover.

Profits from this project will go to the Gulf Coast Writers Association, a non–profit organization dedicated to encouraging and inspiring writers from the Mississippi Gulf Coast region and beyond.

Introduction

Welcome to our 2009 GCWA anthology, *Sweet Tea and Afternoon Tales: New Tales from the South.* Between these pages, you will find another cornucopia of southern tales for your reading pleasures–a blend of new and familiar voices. Our only guideline for this collection was that stories must reflect a truly southern theme and flavor.

The Gulf Coast Writers Association provides a forum for writer–to–writer discussion, publication opportunities, and fellowship. We sponsor this yearly anthology, the magazine *Magnolia Quarterly,* a yearly contest, and many other opportunities for writers. Check us at www.gcwriters.org.

Philip L. Levin and Dixon Hearne, Editors

About the Cover

Barbecue, Picture Hats and Cool Mint Juleps by Alice Moseley.

My mom used to say that this is the print she sells most to the "snowbirds," our friends from Iowa and Minnesota who come in the winter to play golf and eat our oysters and shrimp. Barbecue means different things to people from different parts of the country, but barbeque, in this print, refers to the Memphis definition, a sandwich on a hamburger bun overflowing with pulled barbeque pork and topped off with cold slaw and a sweet barbecue sauce. Picture hats were the topic of one of Mom's funny stories. Her mother's favorite picture hat was left on the bed in preparation for a function later one night when my mom was about 12 years old. My mom said she almost got in trouble on this occasion, for laughing when her mother discovered that the cat had licked all the color off the artificial grapes on her picture hat. Every time my mom told this story, I could hear a special chuckle of enjoyment in her voice. My mom and her mom had a difficult relationship and telling this story would bring a secret little smile of satisfaction to my mom's face, even at age 94. I don't think my mom ever had a mint julep, or knew much about them, but Barbeque, Picture Hats and Mint Juleps as a title, does have a ring to it. –Tim Moseley

Please visit the ALICE MOSELEY FOLK ARTIST Museum in Bay St. Louis, MS

Introduction to Southern Charms
by Marlyn Allgood

Living in Michigan from birth in 1932 until moving to Mississippi in 2000 allows me to consider myself an authority on how wonderful it feels to live in the south. First, it's the honey–dripping accent. Southerners never believe they have accents, immediately noticing yours and asking, "Where ya'll FROM?" Who could look into those big beautiful southern girl eyes, see that warm smile, and be offended by the question?

"Welcome to Mississippi, we hope ya'll have a good visit. Ya'll have any kin around here?" A yes answer could begin the most blessed conversations of the day, when you mention a cousin's name and right away you see a big smile of recognition. Because you see, whoever you meet anywhere in town is going to know your family. They will name names that are familiar to you, tell you where they live, who they went to school with, where they worked, and that their sister is married to one of them, a distant cousin. Following that will be the Genealogy lesson all the way back to your Great Grand Daddy.

Right away, you feel at home. You should. Just picture this: You and your husband have stopped for gas on your first visit to his family in Mississippi. He's bringing you down to show off, you know, the new wife. The second one. The Yankee. Going inside to pay, he notices it smells REALLY GOOD in there. The menu lists Fried Chicken, Cornbread, Greens, Green Beans, Peas, Macaroni and Cheese and last but nowhere near least, there is Peach Cobbler! All this for $4.95, including Sweet Tea. He returns to you and says, "Maybe we should go inside and try the food?" You look around at the muddy trucks and gas pumps, and say, "This is a Cafe?" You give it a try anyway, and discover you love their southern cooking. And, you will even go out of your way to eat there again.

Now, genuine southern Sweet Tea is always served cold, even on those rare winter mornings when a thin layer of ice forms at the edge of the pond. Notice there are no gritty grains of sugar swimming around in the bottom of your glass? Genuine southern Sweet Tea is always perfectly clear and iced to the top of the glass, in fact, some folks actually purchase their ice cubes to guarantee it. It would certainly astonish your Cafe waitress if you were to ask for HOT tea! Instead, just smile, ask for a glass of our Sweet Tea, and make a new friend. Just ask, "Y'all have any kin around here?" You'll be glad you did. Besides, it's the southern thing to do.

Y'all come and see us, now.

Henry and the Naked Ladies
by Shannon Rulè Bardwell

"Do not lust in your heart after her beauty or let her captivate you with her eyes, for the prostitute reduces you to a loaf of bread." Proverbs 6:25–26 NIV

Aunt Bess walked into the kitchen; her arms loaded with groceries. She looked tired and weighted down by more than groceries. Her dress hung loose where she had shriveled in size over the last year. "Been waiting long?"

"No," I replied, "Just got here myself. Let me help you with those." I walked over to help put away the small amount of canned goods, cereal, and other necessities for an elderly woman living alone.

"Aunt Bess, have you heard anything of Uncle Henry? Do you know his whereabouts?"

"No Honey, haven't heard a thing," she answered.

Aunt Bess continued putting the groceries away but I noticed that her eyes darkened and the shadows on her face deepened.

"It's been over a year now, hasn't it?" I asked.

"Yep, 'bout that. I'll make us some tea and we can sit outside and visit awhile. How's my sister doing?"

"Mom's fine," I assured her. "Aunt Bess, I'd like to hear what happened to Henry; you know Mom never told me the whole story. She said he just left one day."

Aunt Bess gathered the teapot, two cups and a plate, a faint smile on her lips. "Well, Child. I think I'm ready to tell you. I don't think before now I could have said. Even though I lived it and saw it happen, it's the strangest story I've ever heard of."

I was eager to hear because never in a million years did I think my Uncle Henry would have left Aunt Bess. They had been married almost fifty years. Aunt Bess put the tea service on a tray with a plate of my favorite lemon cookies and carried them to the front porch. I looked around the yard and noticed the shrubbery was a bit overgrown and Uncle Henry's old fishing boat sat on the side of the house.

We sat down and Aunt Bess started, "Child, this is going to sound crazy to you, but this is what happened. A little over a year ago, I started seeing things ... seeing people in the house."

My eyes widened a bit. "You mean like ghosts?"

"Not exactly, I would see women in the house. They were everywhere. It was kind of scary at first but they didn't do anything. They were just sitting around. I could go about my business undisturbed while they sat there watching."

She took a sip from her tea, checking me out over the rim of her cup. I smiled encouragingly. "Go on."

"Well, naturally I couldn't tell anyone I was seeing people in the house. They'd think I was loony tunes. I was beginning to think I was loony tunes. There's one more thing about the ladies. They were naked."

"Naked? The ladies were naked?" I asked.

"Yes, they were. I thought that was very odd. They were all naked but seemed comfortable in their nakedness. Most of them, one in particular, wore black high heel shoes. She sat on the back of the sofa right there in that living room and bounced her foot up and down. Now that part got on my nerves, her sitting on the back of my sofa and bouncing that foot. You know, Child, there is nothing attractive about black high heel shoes and naked."

I bit my lip to keep from smiling. Aunt Bess was seeing naked ladies in her house and she was bothered that the black high heel shoes weren't attractive. "So what happened to them and what does all this have to do with Henry leaving?"

"Everything, Child. I started seeing these naked ladies just after Henry came home with that computer box. That dad gum computer box was Henry's downfall."

"How was a computer Uncle Henry's downfall?" I asked. The story was sounding more and more bizarre by the minute.

"Well, like I was saying, I was seeing those naked ladies and I couldn't talk to the preacher or the women at the church circle, so one day I happened to run into a woman from the Prophesy Church. We chatted and then I confessed I was seeing the naked ladies in my house."

"She asked, 'What do they look like?' I said, 'They look naked of course.'"

I bit my lip again, "And?"

"The Prophesy lady thought for a minute and said, 'That's the spirit of prostitution. That's who they are. You can read about it in the book of Hosea. That's a hard one and they are not likely to leave easily. You have to exorcise them out.' I wanted to know how that spirit thing got in the house in the first place but she couldn't say."

"How do you exorcise the spirit of prostitution out of your house?" I asked.

"She said put cooking oil on the doors and windows and pray, 'Let the spirit of evil leave this house.' I was supposed to say it seven times. But it didn't work. When I went back to her she said the spirit of prostitution was a hard one."

It felt strange listening to Aunt Bess talking about naked ladies in her house and exorcising spirits. She was very sure about what had happened. I caught myself glancing toward the living room sofa to see if it held any naked ladies in black high heel shoes. There were none. "So what does this have to do with Uncle Henry?"

Aunt Bess continued, "Everything, Child. You see, Henry spent all his time on the computer. He stopped his yard work; he even quit fishing. The only thing he did was go to the church for his deacon meeting. Some nights he didn't even come to bed. He stayed in that back room."

"Every night I'd pray to the sweet Lord Jesus to help my Henry. That computer box got a hold of him and it was a hundred times worse than gambling or alcohol. He didn't even watch television no more. So it was that one night he went to the deacon meeting and I went into the back room where the computer box was. Sally had been sending those email notes and pictures of the grandkids and Henry brought them to me. I wanted to see if I could find the pictures for myself on the computer box. That's when I found the naked ladies. That's how they were getting in, through the computer box. They were taking over my house and my Henry. He was looking at naked ladies on the computer box night and day. There were thousands of them. You couldn't even imagine what all was on that computer box."

"What did you do Aunt Bess?"

"Well, I heard Henry coming in the front door and I hollered at him to come to the back room. I told him that I knew all about the naked ladies on the computer box. I said, 'Henry Hinkle you are a married man and a church man and you have no business looking at naked ladies. They will reduce you to a loaf of bread!'"

"Henry stood there with his eyes all glazed over and pale like he was on dope or something. So I told him again, 'Henry Hinkle, this computer box has got to go and the naked ladies are going, too!'"

"Henry looked at me real mean like and said, 'Don't you touch that computer box,' and then he turned and walked right out the front door."

"I walked over to the sofa and one of those naked ladies said, 'Old lady, we are invited here and we intend to stay!'"

"I walked right up to her and pointed my finger at her nose and said, 'Young lady, I may be an old woman but one thing I do know, and that's black high heel shoes don't and never did look good with naked.'"

I had to stifle my laugh. "So what happened next?"

"Well, a few days later, Henry and the computer box and the naked ladies were gone. That was the last I saw of any of them. I think those naked ladies turned him into a loaf of bread just like the Bible says."

After that we finished our tea and lemon cookies, and I picked up the tray to take back to the kitchen. On the way through the living room a cookie fell off the tray and rolled under the sofa. I sat the tray down on the coffee table and knelt down to retrieve the cookie. Imagine my surprise when I spotted something lying next to the cookie. Reaching in, I pulled out a black high heel shoe.

Barbie and Damon
by Betty Wilson Beamguard

It started when Woody's sister Barbie called on a Friday night, asking for him to come pick her up at the bus station. She'd been out of touch for months after taking off with some no-good drifter named Damon who played guitar in bars for tips. They'd been traipsing all over the country that spring and summer, staying with anybody who'd take them in—relatives, friends, friends of friends.

When Barbie called, Woody asked her straight out about Damon. She swore they'd split up, so Woody jumped in his pickup and took off in the pouring rain while I straightened up the apartment. With me working full-time at the Pay-and-Wash and him doing overtime at Junior Beaver's garage, we didn't do much house cleaning. We figured we were living in a dump, worn-out apartments full of trashy people, so why clean? We were trying to save up for the down payment on a doublewide to put on my grandma's land.

I was still scrubbing on the bathtub when in walked Barbie and Damon both. Mama raised me to act like a lady, and I know how it hurts when Woody's family is rude to me, so I pretended to be glad to see 'em. Wasn't until later, when me and Woody was alone, that I found out about the crying fit Barbie pitched at the bus station after he spotted Damon. It's a wonder he didn't walk off and leave them both down there. Woody hated his guts on account of Damon putting his mama through hell over dating Barbie.

We sat around drinking beer and eating Fritos with them two smoking like campfires. Woody had given up smoking when he started working down at the garage, scared he'd get blown to kingdom come with all that gas and oil around. I was always onto him about it anyway, on account of watching my daddy die of emphysema. But neither one of us said a word about their cigarettes—just watched them puff away, blowing smoke up in the air like they thought they was Hollywood cool.

Around ten thirty, I started dropping hints we needed to get in bed, but hintin' didn't cut it with them. I finally said, "That couch you're setting on folds out. I know y'all are tired after all that riding. Let me go get you some sheets."

I dragged out the old stripedy sheets I hate—the ones in three shades of green Woody's Aunt Tinkie give us when we got married—and held them out. But Barbie and Damon still just sat there. I finally said, "Well, I can't put them on 'til y'all get up."

Both of them looked up with big surprised eyes like they hadn't even noticed me standing there with sheets. They stubbed out their smokes and Woody yanked out the bed. The mice had got in it back when Woody's mama had it, so it smelled, but they were gonna stink it up with cigarette smoke anyway, so what did it matter?

Next morning, Woody got up at six thirty for work, but I stayed in bed awhile. Nothing in the strip mall opened till nine. At eight thirty, when I walked by 'em to get out, they was both still laid up there zonked out with her leg throwed over his, their mouths hanging open, and him snoring like a bull frog. They never moved a muscle, even when I accidentally bumped the corner of the bed frame with the door trying to squeeze out. I bumped it hard, too, and kicked it. Still no movement.

Saturday is our busiest day at the Pay–and–Wash. Weekends is when everybody does their laundry. Wore slap out, I come home, opened the door and found Damon, right where I'd left him. He had the TV on and was all stretched out there with his ankles crossed and his arms folded behind his head like he was king of the world. He grinned that goofy rotty–toothed grin of his with his greasy black hair curling down on his face and said, "Welcome home."

"Thanks. Mind if I stay for supper? Something smells mighty good."

"Don't mind at all."

About the time I got scooted past the end of the bed, Woody come in covered in grease and smelling like a tailpipe, but I've got used to it. It pays the bills.

Damon did the same stupid "Welcome home" routine with him and grinned like he thought he was funnier than Jeff Foxworthy. Woody cut into him with his eyes, cussed when he banged his shin on the bed frame, and headed for the shower.

I went on to the kitchen where Barbie had supper nearly done—fried chicken, mashed potatoes and pork 'n beans, even biscuits. "I could get used to this," I said. She smiled like a little girl proud of her first cookies. She's not much bigger than a little girl and had her blondish hair all chopped off and sticking out every which way.

"I made up some of that chocolate fudge pudding you had up in the cabinet."

"Great!" I dropped down in a kitchen chair and let her do it all. Then we ate and talked and played penny ante poker till bedtime.

Sunday morning, me and Woody got up kinda late, but those two were still passed out. I got out some Life cereal and went for the milk. Wasn't a drop left in the house, Barbie had used it up on the mashed potatoes and pudding. But what can you say? She did fix supper. I fried up some sandwich ham, made toast, and scrambled a couple of eggs. It was kinda nice. I get tired of cold cereal, but I'm too lazy to fix anything else and Woody just plain don't care. Long as its food, he don't complain.

About halfway through breakfast, Barbie came dragging in with that hair standing out like a dandelion gone to seed. She had on one of Damon's T-shirts, which covered everything, but just barely. She set down across from Woody.

I said, "I'm sorry I didn't fix enough for y'all, but you was still sleeping."

"That's all right. I don't do breakfast."

Woody looked straight at Barbie. "What are y'all's plans?"

"Plans?"

"Yeah, like how long you plan on staying here?"

I woulda never come right out and asked like that, but considering their history and considering they was eating from our table and watching our TV while we was out working, I figured he did have the right.

Barbie picked at her way too pink nail polish. "I'm pregnant."

Woody whammed both hands down on the table so hard the plates jumped and us too. "Damn it, Barbie, you little fool. Now what you gonna do?"

"We just need a chance to get on our feet. Find jobs and get a place to live."

"You coulda done been on your feet if you'd kept them in one place for more'n two weeks at a time instead of bumming around all over the country like life was one big vacation."

Her little hands started shaking and she teared up. "We got no place else to go, Woody. Just give us two weeks. That's all I ask. Might not even take that long."

It pure–T turned my stomach to think about two weeks with that couch pulled out, no privacy, the smoke, but he couldn't turn away his own flesh and blood.

"All right, but only because you're pregnant. Two weeks max—and then you're outta here."

We both worked hard to find them jobs. I called Hair It Is, but they needed a licensed beautician, not a shampoo girl. I took her for an interview over at the Wicked Wolf Gift Shop, but they never called back.

Then I seen this ad for light cleaning and give her the number and she called. They was wanting somebody to clean out litter boxes at some kind of cat refuge. This old lady with a big two-story house took in strays to save them from getting killed at the county shelter, and she offered to pay Barbie six dollars an hour to clean out the litter boxes and wash their dishes and feed them all day. She had over a hundred.

Me and Woody teased her like crazy about that, beings how she don't even like cats. Of course with her pregnant, it wouldn't be healthy. Then a thought struck me. That would be the perfect job for Damon—raking up cat crap all day. Talk about the job from hell. "Hey, you could do it, Damon. You're not pregnant." If looks could kill.

I finally found Barbie a job cleaning tanning beds and washing up the towels at the Body Glow tanning place there in the strip mall where I work, which she liked okay. The only one Woody could find for Damon was helping a septic tank guy—an older man that needed somebody young to do the digging for him and run the pumper hose thingy down in there to suck the stuff up.

Woody dropped him off at the man's house that first morning. That night, Damon told Woody he wouldn't have to do that no more, that the man was gonna take him and pick him up from then on. To hear Damon tell it, all the man did was drive the truck and stand around watching him work, maybe talk to the homeowner if the homeowner could stand to stay out there. Then the man took the nice fat check when Damon got done with all the work.

Things rocked along pretty good for a few days. Barbie cooked and I did the dishes. But since neither one of them had got paid yet, we had to buy all the groceries and their cigarettes. That Damon could eat! I told Woody you'd think working over septic tanks all day would kill his appetite, but no such luck.

Then little warning signs popped up. Damon said he wouldn't get paid until the end of the month. Mrs. Pressgrove, the apartment manager, called to tell us the neighbors below us had complained somebody peed off of our balcony—twice in the middle of the day. She'd tried to call about it during the day but got hung up on. She said she knew that didn't sound like us. And the Mexicans next door, a bunch of men that work nights, complained to her about our loud music keeping them awake every day.

"They ain't been nobody here, Mrs. Pressgrove. We got company, but they're gone during the day." She took my word for it and hung up.

Next morning, I noticed blood smeared on the toilet seat and a drop on the bathroom floor. I tiptoed back to the bedroom. "Woody, you bleeding?"

He gave me his dumb google-eyed look. "Do I look like I'm bleeding?"

"I mean where it don't show—like hemorrhoids or something."

"What are you talking about, Girl?"

"There's blood in the bathroom. If I'm not bleeding and you're not bleeding, then it's one of them. I bet Barbie was lying about being pregnant," I whispered.

"She danged well better not be."

We put our heads together and come up with a plan to do some checking. That night, while the rest of us watched TV, Woody shut the bedroom door and called the man Damon was supposed to be working for. He told Woody that Damon went home with a sick headache at lunchtime the first day. Said Damon's wife called next morning and told him he'd been in a bad wreck and might never work again, might not even live. It was all I could do to keep him from tying into Damon right then, but I told him to call 'em out on the balcony to see the stars or have a beer or something. While he entertained 'em out there, I went through Barbie's purse. Found a half-used box of tampons and the dated receipt.

Soon as they come in off the balcony, we said goodnight and slipped off to the bedroom. I told Woody what I found. His eyes got real big, his face turned red, and he balled up his fists. I jumped in front of him to try to calm him down, but he shoved me aside and charged in there yelling like all get out.

"You two low-down no-good freeloadin' ..."

They'd already flopped down on the sofa bed and before they could jump up, he yanked that sheet right out from under them, ripping it down the middle. Tumbled Barbie clear off the bed and over against the wall, and rolled Damon to the middle. They crawled and scrambled around, trying to stay out of his reach while they gathered up their clothes. He was still yelling and waving his arms around when they bumped and banged out the door with their suitcases.

I have no idea how they left town. Last we saw, they was high-tailing it up the street fast as they could go. Woody changed out the lock on the door next day and we never even heard if they was dead or alive until Christmas when we found out they'd turned up on Aunt Tinkie's doorstep.

Baby Dolls
by Lottie Boggan

It was the day after their grandparents' fiftieth wedding anniversary. Most of the kinfolks had gone back home a short while ago, but a few members of the Godbold family who had gathered for the celebration wouldn't be leaving until the next day.

Yesterday morning Mary Margaret and her parents drove in from Gulfport to the old home place in Pike County. She had liked the country. "I might wanta move here," she said to her mother and daddy. But she soon got tired of playing with old timey, flimsy paper dolls, and bouncing on the sleeping porch bed. And she would have no part of blackberry picking or climbing trees.

But last night, going to see other kinfolk for the big fiftieth celebration had been fun. The outfit Mary Margaret wore last month when she won the six-year old division of "Little Miss Harrison County" had been packed for this trip. Her mother dressed her in a white silk blouse with rhinestone buttons, a pale blue satin, body hugging skirt, a pair of tiny, high–heeled denim sandals, and a miniature Kate Spade shoulder bag. As a finishing touch, her mother painted Mary Margaret's lips a bright shade of pink, and shaped them into a Geisha girl pout. "You are your mama's precious little angel, and you don't even look real," she told her daughter. "You should be on the big screen."

At the party everyone told her how pretty she was. One old maid aunt raved, "You look just like somebody's big baby doll. I'd love to stuff you in my suitcase and take you home to Magnolia with me." She made a snorting sound through her nose when she talked. "I'd just prop you up in the corner and look at you."

Mary Margaret could hardly wait to pull away from the aunt's claw–like clutches. Her face was pink and stringy looking, like the ham hocks the maid back in Gulfport cooked with. She reminded Mary Margaret of an old Raggedy Ann doll who had lost most of her stuffing. She had thrown the ugly doll in the garbage just before they came on this trip.

Later, on the way back to her grandparents' home, Mary Margaret and her cousins rode in the back of a pickup truck. The night air was smoother than her feather comforter back home and the overhead stars reminded her of the silver tiara that had been put on her head that night when she was crowned, "Little Miss Harrison County." Summer air whipping past the truck made her skirt flap up. Warm air tickled between her legs and the bouncing motion of the truck rubbed against her bottom. It felt good to Mary Margaret, so propping herself with her hands, she spread her legs, leaned back against the truck's cab, and sank down a little.

But that was yesterday. When she woke up this morning the day was brooding and close and now, in the early afternoon she was so sweaty her clothes stuck to her like a blood–dried Band–Aid.

It was boring out here in the country. A little over an hour ago there had been the rattle of dishes, voices batting one against the other, each person vying for their share of the conversation. Now, the only sounds were the creak of her rocking chair, the high-pitched chatter of her two boy cousins, and every now and then, the clunk and roll of a missed ball on the wooden porch floor.

The last time she had seen her two older Pike County cousins she had only been four, and hadn't paid much, if any attention to them. Now that she had finished the first grade though, for a short time yesterday she had thought they were kind of cute. They reminded her of the "Ken in the Country" doll she had back home. After being with them for only a short while, she changed her mind. They sounded funny, like they were talking with a mouth full of caramel candy. Not only that, they seemed different from her friends back in Gulfport; the cousins had dirt under their fingernails, their jeans weren't Old Navy or Duckhead's, but could have come from Wal-Mart, Penney's, or Sears, and their tennis shoes weren't Easy Spirits, Adidas, or Nikes. And to cap it all off, the boys' faces looked dry and mottled, like the fields on either side of the dusty gravel road leading to their grandparents' house.

"I want my baby dolls," she whispered to herself, "and these cousins aren't any fun." She pushed the rocking chair harder.

"You ain't nothing but a butter–fingered sissy, Walton," Thomas Warren hollered, as the baseball clattered against the side of the house.

A few moments later the front door swung open. "You kids are making way too much racket. We want some peace and quiet," Mary Margaret's daddy said, in a tone of voice that brooked no nonsense or argument. "You boys show your cousin around the farm. We'll freeze some homemade fig ice cream later this afternoon. For now, y'all go on outside and play."

"We have to be nice to her," one of the boys whispered. "Besides, my mama said her family might ask us to spend a weekend on the coast if we're good. They have a swimming pool in their backyard and a big boat at the Broadwater Marina."

Flouncing through the front yard, Mary Margaret ran on ahead of the boys and stood in the shade of a pecan tree waiting until they caught up with her. "There's nothing to do," she complained, flipping her fingers through her hair.

"We can show you our fishing pond," Walton said. "It's right past the barn."

Side by side the three children walked on a well worn path that circled around back of the house, on past a garden and a wooden barn that had shifted to one side, like a jut–hipped woman.

"Come on," the boys called out; now that they had something in mind to show their cousin, they made hot–rod sounds with their mouths as they ran ahead of Mary Margaret. She didn't want to go with them, but neither did she want to be left behind, so she followed. She had to crawl through a barbed wire fence all by herself and even though she held the metal strands as far apart as she could, her dress caught and ripped.

The country cousins ran to a small pond, kicked off their shoes and splashed in the water. Mary Margaret stopped at the edge. To her eyes it was dirty. The pond was small and looked to be the same rusty color as the water that came out of their houseboat lavatory and commodes every now and then. "This isn't fun," she said. "You oughta see our swimming pool in Gulfport. It's not this big, but it's a lot cleaner. The water is bluer than my baby doll's eyes." She spit on her finger and tried to wipe a smudge off her dress. Worrisome insects hummed and lit on Mary Margaret, but they didn't seem to feast on her country cousins. "It's dirty out here and I'm sweating." Earlier in the day her skirt had been stiffly starched. Now it was limp, stained, and torn. "I need my maid to give me a Vita Bubble Bath. I'm hot and sticky. Back home, I have an air–conditioned house, not dumb old window units. This place here smells like our yardman's old shoes." She shook her head irritably, her curly hair a crown of gold circling her round, flushed face.

"We have lots of fun on the coast. There's nothing do to here," she whined. "I play with my Barbie dolls. I've got me a black Barbie doll and I love her just as much as Cabbage Patch Virgie Ann. I've got me an almost live Baby Doll Doe too. She wets. I change her diapers. She cries, and I give her a bottle." Mary Margaret tugged on her skirt and resisted an urge to scratch between her legs. "I just love to take care of little things. I miss my baby dolls. I think my mama and daddy will be ready to take me home soon." She turned around trying to locate her grandparent's house, but it took her a minute to find it. The house didn't look like the same place she had left just a short while ago. Now it reminded her of a monopoly piece and she felt lost.

She plopped her thumb into her mouth.

Walton pointed. "That's gonna make your teeth buck. And once you start first grade, the principal might cut it off."

Mary Margaret took her thumb out of her mouth and examined it. It was wrinkled and ugly, like that old aunt's face. She bent it back and forth against her leg as if she were trying to pop it off. "For your information, I'll be in second grade."

Somewhere on the other side of her grandparent's property, a train blasted out a long, lonesome whistle, the sound trailing away like the cry of her Baby Doll Doe when she laid it down on her bed after giving her a bottle of water. "I bet that train's going to the coast," she said. "I wish I was on it."

"I'm tired of trying to please this brat," Walton muttered to his brother. "I can't swim no how. And even if I could, she ain't going to ask us to her house so we can ride on her silly boat and swim in her dumb pool. It don't matter what we do. I'm tired of hearing how everything's better in Gulfport."

"Try and be nice," Thomas Warren whispered, rolling his lips together. "I wanna go on their big boat." Suddenly his eyes lit up, his face changed. "We got us an old sow pig and she's got eight baby pigs," he blurted out, the pride in his voice overriding the scorn on his brother's face. "They're cuter than dolls. And they're real."

"Oh." Mary Margaret didn't know what a sow pig was, but she had seen piglets in pink skirts frolicking through cartoons. "This little piggy went to market" was one of the first nursery rhymes she remembered. "Pink piggies." The sullen set of her mouth curved into a smile. "Show them to me. I got lots of stuffed animals all over my bed at home. They've got names—Poo Dog, Sugar Baby, Scooby Doo." She hesitated. "But I don't have a little pig."

"They're in a pen. Porker's the mama pig and you can't get too close."

"That's okay. I bet they're just darling little things."

The boys seemed to take on a new energy now that their city cousin was interested in something. They ran ahead of Mary Margaret, chasing each other as she skipped behind them, but this time they waited and held the barbed wire so she could squeeze through the strands. Once under the fence she moved in bouncy steps, like a string–yanked, dancing puppet.

"Come on," the boys yelled. "The pigs are in a pen next to the barn."

Mary Margaret ran behind the boys. When she finally got to the pen, she was out of breath. Her plump face blush pink, she put her hand over her nose, stood stock still and looked into the pen, petrified. There, in a puddle of stinking mud was a huge, fat animal. Mary Margaret had never seen anything like this. The pig snorted and moved from its side to its back. Dangling from its middle were tiny, wiggly creatures who sucked and smacked as they drew from their mother's teats.

"She's just like one of my big old stuffed animals, the dirty one I threw away." Mary Margaret curled her fingers around the frame of the wire gate and sank down, her bottom slipping into mud from the pig pen. "I want a baby pig to take home with me. I'll wash it and dress it, just like one of my baby dolls." Her fingers twisted the stick that held the gate closed. "Look. That one fell off its mama. Come here, baby piggy. I'll be your mama."

"Get away from that gate," Walton hollered. "Pigs is dangerous, especially when they got a litter."

Mary Margaret didn't know what a litter was and didn't see anything dangerous about the cute curly–tailed pigs and their huge wallowing mama. *Taking a piglet would be easy*, she thought. *The mama would never miss just one.* While the boys were talking, she opened the gate, just a crack–then a little farther. She could almost reach the curly screw–tail of a baby pig. The boys would never see her, and then she could hide the cuddly cute pig under her dress. Just another inch. Then she grabbed it!

The piglet squealed, causing the mother to lift her head. The huge sow saw the intruder and let out a roaring grunt. Her three hundred pound body began to lumber toward the opening, scattering nursing piglets as she went.

"What the hell?" Thomas Warren hollered to Mary Margaret. "Get outta that pen," he yelled, making his way toward the gate and grabbing the wire. "Walton! Get a stick–gimme something to beat that pig. Good God a mighty! The pig's gonna get her."

Mary Margaret's screams mingled with shouts from the boys and squeals from the pen full of frantic pigs. The sow roared and charged. Her rolling body that was once so docile became a missile headed for the small girl who held the baby pig's leg much as she would the key to a wind-up toy, not even aware that she still held it. The sow's full body weight hit Mary Margaret, knocking her into the slop and mud. The pig's rasping roar and Mary Margaret's futile screams rent the air. A cloven hoof tore the child's once beautiful dress and slashing yellow teeth glared behind the sow's furrowed snout. She charged again!

"Oh no! Oh my God!" Thomas Warren couldn't look. He dropped the stick and tripped, getting away from the pen. Walton was already ahead of him. Yelling, the boys ran for the house.

At the old home place, the grown-ups rocked, drank coffee and talked about their childhood on the farm. "Just listen to the shrieks from those kids," one said, "seems like only yesterday we were having fun like that."

Mary Margaret's mother smiled. She hoped her daughter wasn't getting dirty. But at least she was playing with other children, rather than just those play pretend stuffed animals and her baby dolls.

Cabin on the Bayou
by Susan Budavari

"Ethan?" A voice came at him from his past.

Charline? He looked over as she closed her wet umbrella and hurried up to where he stood beneath the supermarket overhang waiting for the downpour to end. Five years evaporated. Same look, a few more lines in her brow, same frizzy hair. He stumbled back a step. He wasn't up to a public scene.

"I saw the curly mop." She reached out to smooth his hair. "I hoped it was you."

He pulled back from her touch. "Hello, Charline." Her smile was surprisingly friendly. He didn't smile back.

"A month ago, when your daddy died, I thought you'd come back to Hattiesburg. I expected there'd be a proper church service for him. Wanted to pay my respects but I didn't hear of anything."

"We had something private."

"You know, your daddy and I kept up over the years." She paused and stared over his shoulder in thought. Moving her eyes to meet his, she mumbled, "Well, anyway, sympathies and all that. He was a true southern gentleman."

"Thanks, Charline."

"Stayin' around awhile?" Her tone was bolder.

"Only 'til I sell the house."

She tilted her head. "Got a buyer?"

"Uh–huh."

Her eyebrows shot up. "Aren't you the lucky one? You found someone real quick."

He nodded, searching for anger in her eyes. He deserved it. He'd been no support to her back then. Her loss was huge, yet she'd protected him. "*I don't want both our lives ruined,*" he remembered her saying, despite her anguish. He'd protested, but only for a moment, glad to get away. He'd left her deep in grief—buried his emotions and disappeared.

"Well, where ya stayin'?" she asked.

"In a little motel, ten minutes from here."

She puckered her lower lip and nodded. What she said next caught him by surprise.

"I've missed you."

He didn't react. No sense going down that path.

Tears beaded her eyes. "We still have the cabin, ya know."

"I assumed you'd sold it."

"Thought about it, but couldn't give it up. I go out there alone sometimes. In the stillness I can sit and think... and remember."

He stared at the rain hoping it would stop. "First real rain since I'm back."

"Yeah, only way things cool off this time of year, but ya know that."

He looked down and fidgeted with the grocery sack at his feet. "Do you and Leroy go to the cabin much?" *Were they even still together?*

"We don't. It's empty most of the time."

Glancing at the sky, a feeling of relief came over him. "The rain's let up. Best be going."

"You'll be in town for awhile more, right?"

He nodded.

"You could stay at the cabin. Free. Like I said, it's empty."

He shook his head. I'll never go back to that cabin.

She reached out her hand, lifting his chin until their eyes locked. "Are you sure, Ethan?"

He took her hand, lowering it slowly. "How are things with Leroy?"

"Leroy?" She took a deep breath. "He's my husband, Ethan. We will always love and support each other."

Ethan looked away at the parking lot. "Yeah, Leroy's a good guy. Anyway, I don't think he'd like me hanging around."

She furrowed her brow. "It's been almost five years now. Some people come to terms. Leroy has. I have."

"I guess I haven't," he mumbled.

He tried not to think about that part of his life. But the guilt remained. Guilt that it happened, guilt for letting her take all the blame. He'd hated having to come back, but there was no way around it. He had plans for the money from his father's house. And he had to make sure to get every penny he could from the sale of the homestead, which had been in his family for generations.

"Shame to pay good money on a hotel room. Stay at the cabin." She took a deep breath. "It'd be therapeutic."

Therapeutic! Not the word he'd have used. Torture, maybe. "I'll think about it." He picked up his grocery sack and started to back away.

"Here's my number." She stuck a card in the pocket of his dripping shirt. "Call me and I'll get you the key."

About a month later Charline called. He asked how she got his number.

"I ran into your realty agent, Lydia Henkel," she explained. "She told me the sale on your daddy's place had stalled. One thing led to another and she gave me your number. You don't mind, do you?"

"What do you want from me, Charline?"

"Want from you, Ethan?"

"Yeah." He imagined a hurt look on her face.

"Just thought you might've changed your mind about the cabin. Lydia said you'd laid out a bundle to get your daddy's place in shape. Thought cash might be tight. I wanted to help."

"The cabin? I thought you understood why I couldn't stay there."

"It would help you come to terms."

Maybe she was right. As much as he hated to admit it to himself, if he didn't face his demons, he'd never get past them. He looked around at the peeling wallpaper of his grungy motel room. He'd had enough of being cramped up there. "If I were to stay at the cabin, you'd have to promise you wouldn't come there."

He held his breath, wondering if she would agree.

"No problem."

They met in the little café inside the food mart. He bought himself a black coffee and offered her one, but she declined, holding up her bottle of water. They sat down at a table in a private spot, far away from the only other patrons, two white–haired ladies.

"Look, you can stay as long as you want," she said, sliding the cabin key across the scuffed Formica table top. "It's quiet. You can do your writing. You still write, don't you?"

He nodded. He still wrote—even made enough to live on.

"I imagine you're still working on the next great American novel—or have you finished it?"

"Actually, I mostly write magazine articles. But I have a couple of novels publishers are looking at. I expect to hear back any day now." And that was no lie. His writing was going well. He'd developed understanding and compassion, something he didn't have as a younger man—certainly didn't have five years ago. Now he was able to bring those emotions to the page. People said his writing touched them.

Charline droned on while he sat sipping his coffee, locked in his thoughts. "There's also a TV—with cable," she said. "Cupboard's stocked. We had the cleaners in two weeks ago, so everything's nice and tidy. Leroy and I'd planned to go up this past weekend, but last minute, he had to work."

Ethan looked into her eyes and wondered how different their lives could have been. He'd never felt as strongly about any other woman as he had about Charline. Maybe he'd deluded himself at the time, pretending that their relationship was nothing more than just a fling. He knew he'd loved her little Billy, doubted he could have loved him more had he been his own. But all that was over, five years ago.

"You working, Charline?"

"Yeah, I got my teaching certificate and found a fun job at a nursery school—three and four year olds."

He finished the last of his coffee and pushed the cup aside. "Isn't that tough for you?"

She rubbed her lips together. "How do you mean that?" Then she looked down. "Sometimes. Only if I forget myself." She bit her lower lip. "But mostly, I don't let my mind wander." A tear formed in the corner of her eye. "I love the little ones."

Why had he agreed to meet with her? How could he have thought it would be simple, just get the key to the cabin? *Stupid*.

The look on his face must have betrayed his feelings because she suddenly jumped up. "I'd best be going now. It's not a good idea for me to spend too much time talkin' to you. No sense worryin' Leroy." She pushed her chair out of the way and started to leave.

"Charline."

She turned to face him, eyes open wide, lips parted. "Ethan?"

"Let me pay you something for staying at the cabin." He reached for his wallet.

She raised an open hand. "No money. Just promise me one thing. You'll stay out of the den."

He gave his word, watching her run out of the store.

Ethan drove his dad's ancient Caddy slowly over the unpaved country roads leading to the cabin, memories jumping out at him at every landmark. He wondered how they'd haunt him once he got there.

The cabin suffered from neglect. Rotted boards, chipped paint, and broken screens made the structure appear unlived in for years. The insidious kudzu vines strangled the surrounding shade trees. There was plenty for him to do to pay back Charline for staying there free. Physical labor would help him sweat out his regrets.

He'd brought enough staples to hold him for several weeks. With his laptop computer plus his cell phone he had all he needed to retain a feeling of isolation, yet be able to contact the outside world, should he want to.

His heartbeat pounded as he clutched the key with a clammy hand. Fingers trembling, he unlocked the front door and walked in.

Coming in from the cooler evening air, the sweltering heat inside smothered him. He went through each room opening the windows and turning on the fans. Reaching the last room, he stopped at the doorway determined to honor his promise. He shut the door to the den.

After unpacking the groceries, he settled onto the sofa with a cold beer. Troubling thoughts entered his mind. *If only the school air conditioner hadn't broken.*

Nearly five years ago, Charline had planned their day together at the cabin, weeks in advance. She'd assured Ethan she would have no family obligations that day. Leroy would be out–of–town visiting his mother, and her boy, Billy, would be in nursery school all day. Ethan, completing his Masters in creative writing at Southern Miss, had no obligations of any sort that day. She was already an hour late when he first thought of calling her, and discovered he'd left his cell phone at home.

From the gravel driveway, he had watched Charline's car pull up. She'd gotten out, pressed her finger to her lips and pointed to the back seat. He'd been poised to throw his arms around her, initiating their dance, but instead he just stood there sulking, waiting for her to walk up to him. She whispered, "Billy's nursery school's closed today." She went on to explain, her speech sprinkled with four–letter curses. His feelings, too.

The rendezvous had been her idea and she refused to give it up, despite Billy being there. She said she'd worry later what to tell Leroy and insisted to Ethan that they stay together for a while. Billy could watch television alone in the living room. They'd retreat to the den and lock the door. No problem, she'd announced matter–of–factly. *No problem.* If only they'd thought to lock the *front* door.

During his stay at the cabin, Ethan fell into a routine: each day spent writing for five to six hours, walking in the woods for an hour or so, then puttering around the cabin doing minor repairs for a couple of hours. One morning, he opened the front door and saw her car in the driveway, its engine running, closed up against the oppressive southern heat. He wondered how long she'd been there.

He approached the car cautiously. She lowered the window and stared at him, her eyes red, tears running down her cheeks.

"You promised not to come."

"Its five years today."

He looked at his watch for the date. How could I have let this date get by me? Five years to the day Billy drowned in the bayou, yards from the cabin. *While his mother and I embraced behind the locked door of the den.*

She got out and leaned back against the car door, gazing off towards the bayou.

He reached his hand up, almost touching her shoulder, but then let it fall back to his side. "Do you want to come inside for a moment, have a glass of water or something?"

She shuddered. "That's not why I'm here."

Her swollen eyes focused on him. "I thought long and hard before coming here today. Almost didn't do it. When I got here, I just sat tryin' to decide whether to knock on the door." She pushed away from the car and opened the backseat door. "But I wanted you to see him once."

Ethan bent slowly to peek in. A small figure lay sleeping in a car seat. He studied the child's face. His mouth dropped open. "How old is he?"

"Joshua is four."

She leaned in and smoothed the damp curly mop of hair on the boy's head. When Ethan began to reach out to touch the boy, Charline grabbed his arm. She shook her head as she carefully shut the car door.

He jumped back, startled at her anger.

"Your gift of Joshua made it possible for Leroy to forgive me and for us to go on together. I wanted a second child so badly. Leroy, too. It just hadn't happened for me and him." She took a deep breath and let it out slowly. "We never dreamed that it could cost us our first one."

It caught him off-guard when she threw her arms around him, rested her head on his shoulder for a brief moment then pulled away. "Goodbye, Ethan."

She got into her car. "Mail the key back to me when you go."

Standing there transfixed, he watched as her car disappeared down the road. He spent a long time burning into his memory the only look he might ever have of his son.

Then he walked down to the bayou. He knelt and said a mournful prayer.

His Best Asset
by Linda Chubbuck

The calaboose in Fightingtown Creek, Georgia was not the place Reotis Cobb wanted to wake up in every Sunday morning, but lately the miserable tank had claimed his name as resident pretty often.

He stretched full length on the flop mat that was his bed with his hands laced behind his head causing his arms to fly out like trussed chicken wings. The dark whiskers poking their brittle heads out of his face last night now blossomed like cactus needles in the dark desert of the cell.

His eyes narrowed as he thought how he hated this place. He thought of how fragile a man's liberties had become these days, even after he'd spent the better part of the week busting his ass in the copper mines and sweating like a dumb animal for some foreman who hated his guts. Pullin' a cork didn't use to have its limitations, but somehow lately he managed to find his Sunday mornings worshipping at the Church of St. Mattress in this foul hoosegow. His head was pounding out the truth of too much whiskey and his bloated body sang the praises of nausea and dizziness, a now familiar hymn.

As he swung his feet slowly around and folded them under him in Indian style, he thought of how many Sundays Gran had dressed him up for church in the blue serge pants that were too tight and the short white shirt with sleeves that rode two inches above his wrists. He sneered reflecting on how ridiculous he must have looked as he and Gran walked furtively down the side aisle and sat toward the rear of the church, ready for a hasty exit after the last hymn.

Damn, he was a puny fool back then, a palsied pup that shrunk from the slightest of insults. But things had changed now; he had taken his licks and came up the better man for it.

Through watery eyes he looked at the two other 'guests' with whom he shared all this luxury. Both of them lay passed out, snoring and sending up alcohol fumes like invisible smoke signals. The slat wood floors were stamped with a variety of paisley stains of past fluids, oily and vile. No one should have to be treated like a common cur, sleeping in a hellhole like this. Someone had to do something about it; a man was still a man. Maybe he could make a pitch to the town council to get things changed. Like hell he would.

He eyed the bucket that stood lopsided in the corner and wondered if he had to go bad enough to get up and use it. He did. But as he untwisted his legs from the sitting position and stepped gingerly to the bucket, dodging his roommates, he speculated on exactly what it would take to simply blow this place to kingdom come.

When Sheriff Boot Dillard let him out at noon, he had to suffer the lecture that went with freedom.

"You know Reotis, you're drinking yourself into an early grave here. You oughta be thinking about settlin' down, doin' somethin' productive with your time. Life's too short to waste. Use your best assets."

Reotis surveyed Boot's form. Frayed battle boots, faded jeans, topped off with a kaki short–sleeve shirt with "Sheriff" poorly embroidered over the top pocket. Fresh grease stains punctuated the bulging buttonholes from his hammy neck to his belt. Reotis couldn't help but wonder if Boot had ever been accused of using *his* best assets. Maybe he was just born naturally lazy, fat and short on brains.

"Yep, Boot, yer right," he drawled "Probably need to spend more time at Gran's, find some religion."

"Now there's the ticket." Boot winked, his bug eyes swimming with sincerity.

"Ya know, that calaboose needs some rightin' up in there." Reotis jerked his head in the direction of the tiny jail cell.

Boot turned, slow and deliberate and eyed the dull stonewalls. Sucking his teeth into a meditative cluck, he smiled broadly at Reotis.

"Well, wouldn't be much of a deterrent all fixed up, would it now?"

Reotis stared at Boot and shook his head miserably as he started to turn and walk away.

"Where are you headin' now son?" Boot threw in as if he really cared.

Reotis glanced over his shoulder and shrugged at Boot Dillard. "Goin' to think some productive thoughts just like you said, Sheriff." He sauntered slowly down the dirt road kicking up dust devils with each step.

The thought of blowing up the calaboose obsessed him the rest of the day and gave him a kind of peace of mind. He began to figure the particulars involved in such a mission. How much dynamite, the fuse, weather conditions and mostly how he could get away with it. If he couldn't make a clean job of it, it wasn't worth doing.

Loretta Cobb at seventy-four was as spry as a forty year old on her best day. A woman smitten by the word of the Lord and a long standing revered member of the community, her word was as good as the gold you could take to the bank. And she liked it that way.

Reotis had been her son's boy. The wife ran off to Chattanooga with a pan salesman and was never heard from again, leaving Reotis with Loretta and his dad, Levin. But time saw Levin ship out with the Merchant Marine and but for a few postcards and a little cash now and then, he wrote himself out of the picture.

Loretta took up the yoke and raised Reotis as best she could. And while he wasn't a scholar, he was bright and could use his head when he wanted. He just never wanted.

On the Wednesday after his latest stay in the calaboose, Reotis climbed the steps to Gran's porch and plopped into a wicker chair next to the door. His hand clutched the side of his face and he emitted a guttural moan that sounded like a heifer in labor.

Lured by the bellowing, Loretta hurried outside to find Reotis cleaving to his jaw in abject suffering.

"Well son, what ails ya?" She murmured.

His tormented eyes turned full blue on her and he mumbled through the cotton wad he'd stuffed inside his check.

"Tooth, Gran, bad tooth." He pointed at the bulge on the side of his face.

"Dear Lord," Loretta breathed, "how'd you go and let it get so bad?"

Reotis simply turned his best pathetic look toward her and her heart melted.

"Then come on get up, I'm puttin' ya to bed with some paregoric for the pain till we can get you into Doc Levy tomorrow." She grabbed a handful of the sleeve on his shoulder and hoisted him to his feet.

He went with her docilely, intermittently interjecting a moan of real quality. She maneuvered him into the guest bedroom and went off searching for the paregoric. He lay back on the bed as a smile slid over his face.

When she came back with the brown corked bottle, her face was riddled with worry. He hated lying to Gran, but he had to do what he had to do.

"Thanks Gran," he said taking the spoon and bottle from her "How mucha this?"

"I'd say about three tablespoons from the way you're carrying on here." She smoothed back the long hair that fell into his face. "Rest now, I'll be back in awhile to check on you."

He nodded obediently, unplugged the cork and watched as she closed the door quietly behind her. Popping the cork back into the bottle he stretched out, checking his watch to see how long before Gran returned.

Twenty minutes saw Gran peeking in the door, not to disturb, just to check. He moaned and snored intermittently knowing it played well. As the door shut, he checked his watch to be sure. Twenty minutes to the second and she would be back, a creature of habit all her life. You could pretty much set your watch on Gran's time schedule. Twenty minutes would be enough.

Two tablespoons of paregoric would have put any sick man down for an hour or more, so when Loretta stuck her head in the room a second time twenty minutes later, Reotis knew she was convinced that he was down for the count.

This time when the door clicked, Reotis waited till he'd heard the screen door shut and the squeak of the rocker on the front porch.

Tossing the quilt aside, he checked his watch, sprinted to the window and squeezed out. Twilight was settling in on Fightingtown Creek complete with tiny bugs that zigzagged wildly in a frantic pattern much like Reotis as he dashed in the barn and gathered his supplies from an old barrel. The entire town would be at dinner now, his timing was perfect.

The best track star Vestal County High School ever had moved at full stride toward the cowardly structure of the hoosegow. It stood empty, a testament of man's inhumanity to man and a goodly distance from Boot Dillard's office. But he would fix that testament, really quick now.

Peeking in hastily to be sure of no occupants, Reotis quickly arranged the dynamite on the side facing away from Boot's office. Next, he took the incredibly long fuse and set it into the package. The copper mines had taught him something anyway.

Backing away slowly from the jail, he carefully strung the fuse for almost seventy-five feet. Checking his watch, twelve minutes had passed. He dug deep into his jeans pocket and pulled out a lighter Gran had given him two years ago for his birthday. God love Gran, she always gave the best gifts. Flipping the cover back, he drew a deep cleansing breath and lit the fuse. Vestal County's best again sprinted full stride back to Gran's, his feet barely hitting the ground as his strong legs pumped hard and fast down the road.

The explosion rang full and rich in his ears as he pressed himself back through the window and dove into the bed, arranging the quilt just so. Loretta burst through the door to find her grandson twisted up in his quilt snoring. Her jaw went slack that anyone could have slept through the noise but she guessed a man on paregoric could do just that.

Her allegiance to duty kept Loretta in the house rather than walking off to quench her curiosity. Reotis needed her and she wasn't about to leave him. It surprised her when Boot Dillard shuffled the front porch steps and rapped respectfully on the door. She always made him wait. Hat in his hands, he circled the brim once turning it gently clockwise, when Loretta's image framed the door.

"Boot Dillard, what in heaven's sweet name's goin' on in town?"

Boot lowered his head slightly as if in the presence of royalty. "Well, Miz Cobb," he said "It seems someone blowed up the calaboose down to the last stone, nothin' left but a pit."

"Oh my stars!" Loretta gasped putting her slender fingers to her mouth. "Who would do something like that? Anyone hurt?"

"No ma'am, but we figure someone what had a righteous hatred of the place would be our first suspect. Is Reotis in?"

Loretta put it together quickly. "What do you mean Boot is Reotis in? He's been here all afternoon and evenin' too with a toothache. He's righteous as rain, he is. I checked on him regular."

From behind his Gran, Reotis appeared rubbing his cheek and smelling of fresh paregoric, the cotton wad firmly wedged inside his check.

"Wuz up Sheriff?" Reotis mumbled barely intelligible and flashed Boot his finest pitiful look.

Boot surveyed Reotis as Loretta's grandson stood there looking piteous and miserable, then shook his head. "Someone blew up the calaboose clean down to the ground tonight. You got any idea who it might be?" Boot knew he was walking on eggs. Loretta Cobb's word was gospel so his implications bordered on near blasphemy.

Reotis rubbed the evening shadow that had crept across his face. "Can't say as I do Sheriff, but it's probably someone what hated the place."

"Uh huh," the Sheriff grunted, circling his hat in his hands again. "That's what I thought too." Boot looked from Loretta to Reotis and back again. His instincts felt right but his timing was all wrong. Defeated, he squared off at Reotis.

"Well, I hope that tooth gets better Son," Boot said flatly. "You're real lucky to have your Gran here." And he cocked his head toward Loretta.

"You know, Boot," Reotis said, draping his arm around his grandmother's shoulders. "I just was thinking the same thing. She's my best asset."

The Bicycle
by Ed Davis

"Hey!" I yell from where I stand at the water fountain but the big black kid ignores me. He's thrown his bike down and grabbed mine where I left it parked at the picnic table. Now he has one of his hands on the banana seat and one on the left grip of my hi–rise handlebars.

"Hey, that's mine!"

He straddles my bike, pedals down the sidewalk into the street and takes off. I'm left with his cruddy old junker. You can barely tell it was once red, for all the mud and rust on it. Mine cost a lot. It was all I got last Christmas except for underwear. With the mill closing, Mom told me if Daddy Jim hadn't already put it on layaway, I wouldn't have gotten it. Without it, I'll be stuck on Beaumont Avenue for the rest of the summer. I can hear Daddy Jim holler, "And you *let* him take your bike?"

I'm still a block behind the kid, when he rides right up to the front door of a house with almost no paint smack in the middle of Colored Town. I'm breathing so hard I'm scared I might upchuck as I stop and watch him take my bike inside. I've only ever been to this neighborhood before on Christmas, when I helped Mom bring a bunch of old clothes and stuff up to her friend Alma's house. Today there are millions of flowers in every yard.

I start to catch my breath as I slowly ride up to the house. An old rusty mailbox says Turner. That's when I remember the boy's name: Arnold Turner. Before he'd moved last fall, my best friend Benny Donovan had pointed him out to me one day standing in front of Central Poolroom and told me how Arnold had beaten up Keith Clark, the biggest, toughest white kid at Gardner Junior High. That, plus all the water I drank, makes me really need to pee. Then I remember Daddy Jim's belt.

After parking Arnold's bike on the sidewalk, I tiptoe up three crumbly concrete steps to the door and look into a dark hallway. There stands my bike with no one around. The place smells like liver and onions, so I hold my breath. I have one hand on the grip when a voice booms.

"DON'T TOUCH IT."

I jump like an M-80 just went off. Turning toward his voice, I see Arnold sitting on an old green couch in the living room.

"Git in here."

I walk into the dark room, knowing I might not walk out alive.

"Sit down."

I sit on the other end of the couch as far from him as I can. Now I *really* need to pee.

Finally he says, "I know who your mama is. I seen her up to Alma's. She hates us."

"No she don't. She's grateful to Alma for saving her life back when they were little girls. Mom was going down for the third time in Blue Hole when Alma was coming home from church and jumped right in and ..."

He smashes his fist into his palm. "SHUT UP. You're going home on her bike."

"*Her* bike?"

"She left it at Alma's last Christmas with a bunch of other crap that wudn't worth takin' to the dump. You're takin' it back to her and I'll keep yours."

A light flashes in my head. I realize that piece of junk is my real daddy's old Schwinn, the only bike he had as a boy, the one Mom said he was going to fix up for me before he died. It's so beat-up, I didn't recognize it. My kidneys are now about to bust.

"Now *GIT*."

When Arnold slaps my arm, I shoot off the couch. On the porch, I jump the three steps, hop on Dad's Schwinn, fly down Faulkner, skid around the corner and across the tracks before I feel the wind freezing my soaked jeans. I ride harder and begin yelling all the cusswords I know so I won't cry.

By the time I get home, I'm really mad. Arnold made me piss my pants like a baby, and there's not a mark on me. Daddy Jim is up for his shift by now. He'll take one look, smell me, curl up his lip and go for his belt.

I ride back to Arnold's. The door still stands wide open. Before I can talk myself out of it, I walk right in, see the living room's empty and keep walking down the hall till I see light from a doorway. I can turn around, grab my bike and start to make a run for it, but something makes me walk through that doorway. He has to know I'm doing it, or it doesn't count.

Arnold is sitting at the kitchen with his face bent over a plate eating. The liver smell is suffocating, but I force myself not to gag. He lifts his head and stares at me, holding his fork halfway to his mouth.

"I've come back to get my bike, Arnold."

He glances toward the front of the house. I see he sees my stained jeans. "Take it. I's just jokin' you, anyway."

Before I can think of anything to say he says, "I bet you don't even know that Alma is my mama."

"Then why don't you live with her?"

"Only Ezra's kids live with her."

"Oh." That's all I can think of to say.

"Your mama feels sorry for Alma," he says.

"She just wanted you to get a bike for Christmas. That's why she brought you the—"

"Nigger's bike," he finishes for me.

I sucked down air, like after the belt's first whack. "It was my real daddy's bike when he was a little boy."

"Then why didn't he give it to *you*?"

I blush bright as a tomato. *Because I never knew him. Because he died blocking up the foundation of his sister Rosalie's trailer before I was a year old. Because my mother gave his bike to another boy.* I finally let my breath out real slow. "Arnold," I say, "you can have my bike. For keeps."

"Why?" Some of the meanness comes back into his face.

"Because I want my dad's."

His eyes get as big as bike reflectors. He lays his fork down and looks over my shoulder. For a second I think someone is standing behind me. Nothing moves but the curtains in the window. The breeze dries some of the sweat on my face.

The chair screeches when he stands up, and I jump. He's even taller than I remember. I stand up as straight as I can. If he beats me up, I can tell Daddy Jim I did my best not to let one of the gypsies take my bike.

"Take it," he says. "I don't need it now."

He walks right by me and through the doorway. In seconds, I hear the stairs squeaking.

In the hallway, I run my fingers over my bike's sissy bar, across the long, cool plastic seat and up and down the horseshoe handlebars. Will I recognize it if I see it lying in the snow next December?

Outside, I can't believe how dark it's gotten. I wipe my forehead. I'm all tickly inside, like the time Benny and I cut our hands and held them together so our blood could get inside each other. For the millionth time I wish he hadn't moved to Wheeling. Looking down at the bottom of the steps, I see the Schwinn. No fenders, no chain guard, no nothing. But I don't care, not even about the whipping I'm going to get. And the stain on the front of my jeans feels like it goes all the way to the bone.

Magnolia Veil
by Lucy J. Dixon

When I was a girl growing up in the South, summer was celebrated as the children's season. As temperatures soared so did the spirits of those who were shed of school and schedule. Rich or poor, we were outdoor creatures basking in hot breezes on empty playgrounds or lying in cool moss at the bottom of the bayous that snaked through town. Parched days created thick dust from unpaved streets coating everyone's feet, shod or bare. The dust crept into the folds of clothes like powder in the creases of an old woman's face. It was in my tenth summer that the veil of this gritty veneer lifted to reveal a miracle.

There were two air conditioned buildings in town. One was the courthouse, which sported a soda machine where for a nickel and a penny I could buy myself some relief from the heat. The other was the movie theater where every Saturday I sat shivering through the matinee until I stumbled out, blinded by sunshine. One Saturday as I exited the theater, I bumped right into Martha Magee as she walked by. I mumbled my apology and started to run off but feeling somewhat obliged asked her if she was alright.

"Sure, no harm done," she called over her shoulder as she strolled off.

My gaze followed her with interest. Martha was a local girl from the wrong side of the tracks whose infamy preceded her just as much as her protruding stomach did. Martha's pregnancy was conspicuous by the lack of a wedding ring.

"Either you have a husband or you don't have children. Period." My mother had declared.

Women whispered her name and men rolled their eyes and hid behind their evening newspapers. No one knew who the father was and Martha wasn't saying, even though she kept a very high profile during each afternoon's sojourn. No matter the temperature, Martha made a daily appearance in the middle of town.

Martha's walks were the topic of dinner conversations in many a home. I recall Mother saying that it seemed to her that Martha was just plain advertising walking around like that. My father's reply was that it looked like she'd already done some advertising. I listened quietly so to encourage more gossip but that was usually the point when Mother would shush my father.

After our encounter I began secretly joining Martha on her walks. My considerable curiosity made her an irresistible target. I recognized an opportunity to learn all the mysterious secrets of womanhood. Neglecting my manners, I questioned her shrewdly.

"How did she get the baby in her stomach? How was she going to get it out? Did she want a girl or a boy? Why was it so doggone important for her to be married?"

She'd smile and gently shove me away, saying I was too curious for my own good. She was a pretty good sport even when I told her I'd had a fight with my best friend, Leigh Ann, about whether Martha had worn holes in her shoes. I told her I stood up for her and said that her shoes weren't that cheap. I waited eagerly for Martha's response, hoping she would reward my loyalty by showing me the soles of her shoes but she just laughed.

In retrospect, I think she enjoyed my company. I felt sorry for her but she told me not to waste my time. She said folks would talk about her whether she stayed indoors or not and she needed the exercise. By early August her walk was a waddle. Everyone had formed their own suspicions about the father, someone who must have spent every afternoon laying low.

I don't know if it was the oppressive weather or that parents were ready for school to start, but by mid August the grownups in town were becoming increasingly snappish. Fuses were short and reasons for being relegated to the yard were numerous.

After lunch one day Mother left the house to run errands. She wore her customary hat and gloves in spite of the heat. I was left alone at home with the strict instructions to stay in the yard and not to talk to "that Martha person."

Busy making handprints in the dry, powdery dirt I almost missed Martha as she walked by. I sprang to my feet and ran over to the iron fence that surrounded our house. Balancing on the lowest rungs of the fence I waved to her retreating figure. Martha appeared to be in no mood for chitchat today. Disappointed, I returned to my artwork when I was startled by a small cry. Martha was leaning with her hand against a light pole. She was staring at the ground between her feet.

"Hey, Martha, what's wrong?" I called as I ran around the fence and through the gate to her side.

She looked at me, her eyes wide, and gasped, "My water's done broke."

Water? What water? I stared, fear creeping up the back of my neck.

"Go call my ma and tell her to come get me quick."

Water?

"Hurry up!"

I flew up the front steps to the phone. It was a heavy black appliance that resided on its own little shelf in the hall. I jerked up the receiver and pulled the dial all the way around to the "o."

After what seemed like forever, the operator came on the line. I started to tell her about Martha, but she interrupted with, "What is the number you are trying to reach?"

"Hold on." I ran to the porch. "Martha, what's your phone number?"

Martha stood with one arm around the pole and the other holding her stomach.

"She's at home. Call her at home."

"What's your phone number?"

"4272!"

"4272, 4272, 4272." I raced back to the phone.

The operator connected the number, but no one answered.

"Would you like to try another number?" asked the operator.

I turned to run back to Martha and yanked the phone off the shelf with a violent crash. I stared at it in horror.

"Operator ma'am, please be there." Thankfully, the phone still worked.

I ran out shouting, "Your mama's not home. What do I do now?"

Martha had sunk to a sitting position on the sidewalk. "Hurry up! Try the pecan factory. That's where she works." As I turned toward the house, she frantically called, "I don't want to be having this baby right here on the street!" *Yeah, you and me both.* After being assured the folks at the pecan factory would locate Martha's mom and send her to my street, I returned to find her sobbing loudly. The combination of dirt and tears left muddy tracks down her cheeks. I squatted down beside her and waited. Martha's tears began to subside and she soon fell into a curbside stupor.

An occasional screen door squeaked but no one appeared. Martha sitting there on the sidewalk began to weigh heavily on my mind. After some minutes of considerable internal debate, I said, "Um, do you want to wait for your mama in my house?"

She rallied a bit at the offer. I helped her to her feet and led her to our gate. With one arm around her and one pushing from behind, I struggled to get her up the steps and into the house. We stood momentarily in the darkened hallway uncertain what to do. Then she asked for a glass of water.

I returned with a sloshing glass only to find her balanced precariously on one of mama's delicate lady chairs. "Do you suppose I might lie down, if it's ok?"

"Sure, it's ok." I said, pretty sure it was not ok.

I steered her into my bedroom hoping Mother would appreciate that I'd had the good sense not to put her on Mother's bed.

Martha lay still for a moment, melting slowly into the softness of the bedspread. Then suddenly tears began pouring vigorously from her red rimmed eyes. "I want my ma!"

I quickly found a handkerchief and handed it to her. "How about some more water?"

"No thanks."

I started to sit down, but she stopped me.

"Maybe you'd best wait outside. Watch for my ma."

"But..."

"Get out! This ain't the time for your nosy questions!"

Dang!

Standing on the porch, I looked up and down the street for any sign of a grownup. The street was empty except for Martha's shoes lying where she had kicked them off. I ran to pick them up and turning them over, was relieved to find there were no holes in the bottom. I carried them to the screen door and opened it.

"Martha? I've got your shoes. You want 'em?"

There was no response so I placed them just inside the door and returned to the yard.

The afternoon wore on as I continued my vigil, drawing designs in the powdery dirt, sometimes with my hands and sometimes with my toes. My ears were constantly pricked for any sound coming from the house. I thought about going to a neighbor's but I wasn't sure how Mother would react to my bringing Martha into the house and then announcing it to the neighborhood.

When I finally caught sight of Mother, she was stepping down the sidewalk with only the faintest hint of perspiration. I ran up excitedly telling her about Martha.

"Honestly, Dear, I'm not even in the house yet and you're bombarding me with racket. Give me a chance to sit down and catch my breath."

"No, Mother, listen! It's important. Before you go in, I've got to tell you what I've done!"

Mother stopped and gave me the eye. "Well?"

I hesitantly, clumsily, explained the situation.

Mother took an involuntary step backwards. "You let that girl into our HOME?"

My stomach lurched. "What else could I do?"

She stared at the house, then at me, and then returned her gaze to the house. "Well, what am I supposed to do with her?"

I hadn't expected that. Mother was supposed to know what do to. Her words rang in my ears like clanging bells.

She was still for a long moment and just when I thought I'd have to haul Martha back out to the street, she snapped, "Stay put!" She squared her shoulders and marched into the house.

I followed her to the steps and stood waiting for Martha to be booted out but all was quiet. I returned to the tree. Folding my legs under me, I slapped the earth with the palm of my hand over and over sending tiny jets of dust flying up into my eyes.

The afternoon became golden as the sun began its downward journey. Shadows lengthened and the air grew heavy and stagnant. Questions darted around my brain like a wild bird newly trapped in a cage but obedience kept me rooted to the ground.

I looked up to see a short, rotund woman rushing down the sidewalk, flowered dress billowing around her legs.

I jumped to my feet. "Mrs. Magee?"

She sailed over in my direction. "Yes, yes, I'm Mrs. Magee. Do you know where my Martha is?"

"She's here. She's inside."

Without another word she bustled up the steps, grasping the railing and breathing hoarsely. She opened the screen door without knocking and disappeared inside.

I ached to follow her. I strained my ears but ... silence. Later, I heard mother's voice on the telephone. Nothing more.

Time seemed endless as I swung back and forth, back and forth on our iron gate. My hands smelled of rust and my stomach had begun to grumble. I looked up to see Doc Henley puttering up the street in his ancient Bellaire. It was common knowledge that Doc H. had delivered every child in town for the last forty years, including seven babies of his own. He shrugged himself out of his car and slowly climbed the steps. He entered the house also without knocking.

I followed this time and stuck my head in the screen door. I thought about offering to boil water or something but I decided I was in for it enough already.

The church bell rang the six o'clock Angelus and soon Daddy came strolling up the walk. I rushed to tell him the news.

"You say that Martha Magee is having a baby in our house? At this very moment? Imagine that, and good old Doc Henley here in her hour of need. Well, I'd just be in the way. Tell your mother I'll be at the office. Maybe stop by the diner for a sandwich. You want to come?"

I struggled for a quick minute over going to the diner with Daddy and missing this opportunity of a lifetime. "No, I better stay here in case they need me."

Daddy ruffled my hair and told me to keep out of the way; then turned on his heel and headed back downtown. He'd made the right choice. This was no place for a man, I thought as I resumed my swinging on the gate.

The sky darkened and the air cooled slightly. I moved to the porch swing and wrapped my arms around my legs. The street lights turned on, inviting bugs, but I sat in shadow. No one turned on the porch light.

My eyes grew heavy and I dropped my forehead to my arms. It felt like a dream when I heard the faint sound of a baby's cry. I sat up, my heart quickened, and I ran to the door.

Voices were coming down the hall. Doc Henley and Mother walked to the door.

"Keep her here tonight. See if you can get her to eat something. I'll call again in the morning." He walked onto the porch and slowly stretched his back. "You've done a mighty kind thing today, Patricia." he said over his shoulder. Then he went down the steps and squeezed himself back into his car. The engine roared to life and after he drove away, the night sank back into silence.

"Have you been out here all evening?"

I spun around to face Mother, nodding expectantly.

"Would you like to see the baby?"

I nodded again.

Taking my hand she led me to my bedroom. My bedside lamp cast a halo of light on the bed. The air smelled of sweetness and sweat. Mrs. Magee was sitting by Martha talking in a low voice. A tiny bundle lay next to Martha. I looked at her and she said, "She's a girl."

Mrs. Magee stiffly rose and beckoned me closer. I tiptoed over; my hands clasped tightly over my heart for fear the pounding would frighten the baby.

I couldn't see much, she was so bundled up. Her eyes were closed and she looked like a baby doll sleeping in her mother's arms. I lifted my gaze to meet Martha's. My heart fairly burst at the sight of mother and child.

Mother suggested a cup of coffee and she and Mrs. Magee left together. I glanced around the room for signs of the miracle, the mystery of childbirth. But it was just my room, same as always.

"Can I touch her?"

Martha unwrapped the blanket a bit. I knelt on the floor next to the bed and held the baby's tiny hand. We didn't speak and soon Martha's eyes closed. I slipped quietly from the room and went in search of Mother. I found her with Mrs. Magee sitting in the parlor. I stood quietly by the door. The parlor, off limits to me, was used only for special guests. On a little table in front of the settee was a pot of coffee and two unused cups. In their hands rested tiny glasses of amber liquid, which they sipped at intervals.

Mrs. Magee sighed. "I want to thank you for everything. Without your help I hate to think …"

"Please," Mother interrupted, "don't thank me." She glanced toward me in the doorway. "I have a confession to make. I'm ashamed to say that I've spoken unkindly of your daughter."

Mrs. Magee held up her hand. "Don't say another word. I know all about what folks been sayin'. I'm not proud of what she's done." She stopped and closed her eyes. "But you know, there's certainly no sin in that sweet baby's face."

Silence fell over the room. Mother set her glass on the table. She stood and walked past me out of the room. Uncertain what to do I stood in the doorway and watched Mrs. Magee. She sat very still, then turned her head and smiled at me. She gestured me to come into the room. I walked to her side and she reached out and held my hand. Just that—held my hand.

Mother returned with something wrapped in tissue paper. She opened it so that I could see what was inside. I looked at her and eagerly nodded. She handed the package to me and I placed it on Mrs. Magee's lap.

Mother said, "I made it for my own baby ten years ago."

Mrs. Magee opened the rustling tissue and drew out a delicate pink crochet baby blanket. After a moment, she looked at Mother, eyes shining.

"Oh, no, this must be very dear to you, ma'am."

Mother smiled, "I was saving it for a grandchild. I want you to have it for yours."

"Please, it's too fine," protested Mrs. Magee.

But Mother was not to be budged and in the end Mrs. Magee carefully tucked the package under her arm and thanked us profusely.

After checking on Martha, she said she would return the next day. We walked her out on the porch and watched as she made her way to the end of the street, walking in and out of the glow of the street lamps, until she disappeared around the corner.

Mother eased down onto the porch swing and pulled me down next to her. I lay my head on her lap. We ended the day in silence, sharing the evening as it deepened into night. As I drifted off to sleep, a single tear splashed onto my cheek and warmed the chilly darkness.

Voodoo Bayou
by Fred Farris

"I'll give you a dollar and a quarter for the whole batch of 'em," Mr. George, the balding storekeeper, bellowed, looking down at Phillip in disdain.

Phillip bit his lower lip and straightened his torn T-shirt. All his hard work, a full day's catch of catfish and carp from the bayou lay in his hand-cart; almost fifty pounds. Phillip searched the storekeeper's gaunt face, eyes oddly sunk almost like they were scared of the light. "Is that the most you can do Mr. George? That's only two cents a pound."

It was 1940 and most working men, if they were lucky enough to have a job, made only two dollars a day in the bayou parishes of Cajun Louisiana.

"If you were a member of our Brotherhood you'd get an extra five percent bonus for all your fish," the storekeeper said.

"Brotherhood?" Phillip asked.

"Yeah, we help each other find guidance through business and spiritual help."

"Spiritual help? You mean it's a kind of a church?"

The store owner grinned. "Yes, we're called Wiccans. We meet here at the store on Saturday nights."

"Do you do weddings in your church?"

"Sure, we call them Handfastings. The bride and groom hold hands tied together with colorful ribbons. It's a lovely ceremony with vows to each other and to our ways."

"Oh?" Phillip waited.

"Tell you what," the storekeeper added. "I'll give you a dollar and a half for this batch; that's an extra quarter, and you think about coming to one of our meetings. You'd like the folks here."

"Well, I'll think about it, but I ain't saying I'll come for sure."

Phillip pocketed the money he needed for Maria. He thought of the first time he had seen her, sleeping in the bottom of his cousin's rowboat. She opened her eyes when he spoke, and Phillip swore two brown doves flew out. She smiled. He knew he had to see her again.

A carpet of pine needles crunched under Phillip's thin sandals as he turned away from town toward the bayou. A thorn of shame pricked him when the women pointed at him, when they talked of Maria behind her back. Pausing at the white wooden church, he hesitated, bowed his head and stepped inside. Old Father Budeaux entered the confessional booth as if reading Phillip's mind.

"Bless me Father for I have sinned," Phillip said.

Through the thin porous screen he saw the priest rest his chin against his fist like the famous statue "The Thinker." The back of the priest's ancient hand ran rivers of blue through its spotted skin.

He won't understand, he's too old, Phillip thought. His tongue felt useless. Then an almost holy aura gave him courage. "Maria's going to have a baby. Will you marry us Father?"

The moment the priest answered, Phillip crossed himself and bolted from the church like a racer. He ran past the sawmill where he'd worked last summer. An earsplitting whine screamed as a whirling saw–blade sliced through a pine log. He'd heard that same whine, mixed with his own scream a year ago when that saw-blade sliced off three fingers of his left hand. He cringed as he remembered the sight of his severed fingers dropping in the sawdust like three small sausages oozing red. It had taken months of re–learning to use his remaining thumb and forefinger to grip the thick oar of his boat.

Phillip ran alongside an old freight car, now abandoned by the railroad on one of the side tracks. His Cousin Bobby's family lived in the rusting boxcar now. "What's your hurry?" Bobby yelled.

Phillip flashed a grin and a quick wave. He angled to his right on a dirt lane under a canopy of cypress branches and headed toward a small frame house next to the bayou.

Maria opened the torn screen door and stepped out even before he knocked. Her tawny pupils made little stars. He extended his damaged hand up and cradled her chin between his thumb and forefinger. Maria kissed its scars and looked up into his eyes.

"Father Budeaux said yes," he blurted.

Maria burst into tears. "I love you Philly." Her praline sweet voice always went into his heart; his gut. Now they'd have a proper wedding in church. No more public shame. Maria's cousins would be both jealous and happy.

"It will be a boy," Phillip bragged, "and I'll teach him how to fish." He lifted her small left hand to his lips and kissed Maria's naked ring finger.

"I'll put a real gold wedding ring on this finger."

"Wonderful! Then I'll be Mrs. Phillip Landrey." Her auburn hair bounced as she jumped up and down. Most of Maria's cousins didn't have wedding rings these days. Some borrowed their mother's ring if she had one, then gave it back.

Hand in hand Phillip and Maria watched a blue heron step his long legs over to a new fishing spot. A lone loon added an oboe solo. An amber sun slipped below the bayou horizon.

The bayou used to offer up more of a living for a man willing to troll her day and night. This year, however, a marine blight invaded local water. Some called it a voodoo curse. Fish were dying. The survivors were smaller than the fat twenty–pounders common in years past, and now Phillip needed money for their engagement party. It would be the customary pig roast so neighbors would see Phillip could provide for his new family.

He also needed money for Maria's ring he had promised.

"Let's get married next Sunday," Maria cooed.

"Good, then we'll have the pig roast on Saturday."

Phillip fished from dawn to dusk every day, still he only had enough money for the pig roast. Not for the ring.

Cousin Bobby arrived early on Saturday. "Let's chop more logs. We need a really big fire. It's got to burn all day," Bobby said.

The two men piled pine logs as high as their belt buckles. They prepared a seventy-pound porker, struggling to clamp the whole pig between two metal farm gates like a giant pork sandwich. Two more neighbors helped lift and hang the hulk beneath iron poles forming a tent-like frame. Then the four master chefs maneuvered the heavy pig-rig over the log pile.

Mr. George chugged to a stop in his black Model–A Ford and stepped out.

"I see you're going to have a Balefire," the storekeeper said, looking at the rig.

"It's a fire for our pig roast, our wedding party," Phillip said.

"Have you thought any more about having a Wiccan wedding?"

"Thanks, but Father Budeaux's going to marry us."

"Oh?" The storekeeper's eyes seemed darker, ominous, like a jilted suitor. He stomped back to his car and sped away trailing dust.

"Watch out for that guy," Bobby warned. "I went to a couple of their meetings. They're witches ya know, and he was making a Qureant."

"A what?" Phillip asked.

"A Qureant. Its questions they ask about you before casting a spell, and a Balefire is their fire ritual."

Phillip remembered old talk about some strange pagan rituals when he was a kid. The tales had spread like kudzuvine through the bayou.

"What a bunch of crap," Phillip said. "But don't tell Maria, she'll worry."

They lit the fire before noon, so by dusk glowing coals shimmered upward, enveloping and simmering the charring pork. Each quarter-hour two guys rotated the metal gate to a new position. All afternoon neighbors came by to slap Phillip on the back and slather the pig with long handled brushes dripping with spicy-sweet vinegar and Creole red pepper sauce. Pork fat and sauce dripping on the fire sizzled, crackled and smoked the roasting dinner all day long.

An hour before sundown people began arriving. The smells of barbecue smoke, burnt wood, and charred pigskin floated over the twilight.

Father Budeaux pronounced it all, "An ethereal essence."

Cajun chef friends with freshly sharpened Bowie knives sliced deep through the skin to cut slices from the pig's burnt blackened ribs. Crispy barbeque, skin and all scorched eager fingers. Sorghum molasses on golden cornbread yielded tastes of heaven. Other neighbors brought crawfish jambalaya with tasty "dirty–rice dressing" and homemade rice beer.

Father Budeaux removed his collar, loaded his plate again and proclaimed, "No greater pleasure upon the palate of man."

Maria, in her orange skirt made from cloth of dyed chicken-feed bags, swirled as she danced, never seeming to tire.

A Jew's harp's nimble twang harmonized with a happy harmonica. A frisky fiddle and French concertina blended folk-tunes, ragtime and country blues in a Cajun cadence. Serpentine melodies curled around dancers' feet. Girls flirted then looked away. Boys nodded and smiled, not looking away. Passionate chords entered their veins like the sizzling meal. Phillip and Maria rocked to the rolling rhythm, and the beat came from their pounding hearts.

Grandmas and grandpas stomped in circles with little kids. Teenagers two–stepped until well after dark as their shadows flickered on and off pine trees.

By ten o'clock, most everyone had sauntered toward home. Phillip drew Maria aside. "I'm going to fish all night to get more money for your ring."

"Be careful," she pleaded, with a long moist kiss.

Leaving Maria with his Cousin Bobby, Phillip headed for his rowboat. The water close in front looked like black silk with tiny silver ripples. Phillip drove the wide oars into its darkness as the prow parted the water on a final mission before the next day's wedding. The night was cool and happy.

A night loon moaned. A dead fish scale glinted on the bayou from the moonlight. The black shadow of a muskrat slinked along the shore; a robber on the run. The muskrat reminded Phillip of the storekeeper who a couple of weeks ago had shown him a tray of gold rings and crucifixes kept in a carefully locked case. "I can pay you half down today for a ring and give you the rest in a couple weeks," Phillip had offered.

But the greedy man countered, "Leave me your boat as collateral."

Wouldn't that be like hocking his soul to the devil? His boat, his father's boat before him, was the one thing of value Phillip owned in this world. A man with a boat can promise a woman she will have food for the table.

Phillip hung a coal–oil lamp over the boat's side hoping the light would lure fish. He always mouthed "Thankee Lord" when he landed a big one. Tonight he hoped more than ever for a big one.

In the moonlight he struggled to bait his hook with a crawdad. The whish of his fishing line whipped forward. Its sound reminded Phillip of his French grandfather's tale about the lash of a whip cracking over bare–backed workers on a Martinique sugar plantation a hundred years ago. The repeated whish–whish caught at his soul as Phillip cast out into the dark. It also made him think of old voodoo curses some folks still believed, even to this day about this bayou; the story about a young girl disappearing and the one about a midnight murderer.

The dank dark covered Phillip's head like a damp veil. A mildew odor crept out of the mist reminding him of things better forgotten. Suddenly the black night showed its teeth in a flash of silent summer lightning.

A full moon shown through an opening between the dark clouds, it cast dark shadows from overhanging tree branches onto the water. Shadowy lines on the water transformed into the snake–whip his grandfather had described. *I'm not going to let that mumbo–jumbo of the storekeeper poison my mind.* With a flick of his expert arm Phillip plopped a crawdad into the center of the watery apparition, shattering it into shards.

A soft splash of an oar dipping in the water came from his left, or wait! Was it behind? There it was again ... or was it his imagination? Who else would be out on the bayou at night? Especially this dark night. "Don't think about it," he told the night. *Just think about my wedding to Maria tomorrow.*

Only a few small fish fell for the lantern's lure. A dreary dawn hung silent gloom over Phillip's meager catch.

Early sun fingered through trees. A fat water spider skimmed along the surface; choice bait for carp. Phillip grabbed into the water, closing his fingers around the spider. A stabbing needle prick of pain burned his wrist. An olive–green water moccasin, the size of a fat water hose, slithered away. Pencil–thin snake babies wiggled behind their mother, disturbed from their nest.

Two fang punctures showed on his wrist. He must stop the venom from going up the arm toward his heart. With his knife, he cut an X slit into each fang mark. He sucked his wrist and spit. A purple swelling rose and inched up his arm. He sucked and spit again. Phillip grabbed the bandana off his head and made a tourniquet around his arm above the bite.

Don't panic, try to relax, physical activity speeds up the pulse carrying venom to the heart. This he knew, so it ruled out rowing fast for home. Waves of nausea made him throw up. I can't pass out. What would happen to Maria ... to her broken heart?

Reaching into the water Phillip gathered swamp weed, made a poultice, and put it on the spreading purple veins.

A swamp owl screeched close overhead, but its normal loud hoot was barely audible. Phillip slapped his head with his hand...was he slipping? His muscles felt weak ... more nausea. He washed out his mouth from his canteen; spit, and gulped water. He sucked on the wound and spit again. Then he lay back in the boat bottom so he wouldn't fall into the water.

A high noon sun burned his face as he regained consciousness. He sat up and stared at his arm. The purple had almost gone. "Thank You God," Phillip said out loud, making sure he could hear his own voice.

His fishing line off the stern bobbed under and under again. Had he snagged one last big one before heading home? If not, Maria would be disappointed about having no ring, but she'd understand. Wouldn't she?

As he reeled in the line, a small carp dangled from it; maybe only three pounds but still a keeper. He swung the fish into the boat and grabbed it firmly through the gills to force its mouth open and remove the hook. Deep in the fish's yawning gullet something glinted in the sun. *Another hook? Poor other unlucky fisherman.*

Reaching his fingers down the carp's throat, Phillip yanked out the object. He stared in disbelief! A ring ... a gold ring, an honest–to–God gold wedding band. Had God slipped it off a fellow fisherman's finger and into the mouth of this deliverer?

Phillip Landrey laughed out loud; tilted his head back and bellowed, "THANKEE LORD" at Voodoo Bayou. He kissed the wiggling carp; kissed his bride's wedding ring. Then he pulled his oars through the thick noon water toward the church and Maria.

Appearances
by John M. Floyd

He drew a shaky breath and punched in the numbers. His mouth was as dry as sandpaper when he heard her pick up the phone.

"Yvette?" he said. "It's Tommy."

A silence passed, "Who?"

"Tommy Bridges. I sit beside you in chemistry."

He heard slurping sounds, and finally realized she was chewing gum. Somehow that made him feel better. The image of perfect, golden-haired Yvette McKenna smacking away on a wad of Juicy Fruit made her seem more accessible, more...human. To the rest of the high school she was head cheerleader and prom queen. To Tommy Bridges she was a goddess.

"So?" she asked, smacking.

He swallowed. "Well, there's a big concert downtown tonight, and—"

The chewing sounds stopped. "ZZ Top? You got *tickets?*"

"Five rows from the stage." He almost revealed that he'd bought them at half price from his flu–stricken cousin Edward, but caught himself just in time. "Will you go with me?" he added, holding his breath.

Another long silence. "Maybe."

"Maybe?"

"Call me again at one o'clock."

Tommy exhaled. "One this afternoon?"

"No, one tomorrow morning, Bridges. Of course this afternoon." The smacking had started up again. "I'll tell you then whether I can go."

"Ah ... okay. I'll call you at one." There was no reply— she'd already hung up the phone.

Tommy replaced the receiver and sat looking at it, dazed. He decided it didn't matter much that she hadn't said yes. What mattered was that she hadn't said no.

He was still staring at the phone when it rang again. He almost jumped off the chair. The caller, it turned out, was his friend Rufus Landers, asking if he wanted to go to the state fair. Tomorrow was the last day.

Tommy hesitated. He wasn't wild about the fair right now, but if he stayed around here waiting for one o'clock he'd go insane. He agreed, pulled a sweater over his head, and checked the two precious concert tickets he'd tucked into his wallet. Remembering Yvette's apparent fancy for chewing gum, he found a stick of Doublemint and put it in too, just in case, beside the tickets. Pleased with himself, he stomped downstairs and out the front door. He still felt a little giddy, as if wandering around in a dream.

Maybe it *was* a dream, he told himself. *Yvette McKenna.*

He felt a twinge of panic. How exactly should one act, on a date with a girl like Yvette? He remembered the old joke about the dog that, after chasing cars all his life, finally caught one and then didn't know what to do with it.

Tommy was so preoccupied he almost didn't notice Lizzie Kelso, who was raking leaves in the front yard of the house next door. The Kelsos' lot was thick with pecan trees, and even though cool weather had barely begun here in the South, pecans always shed their leaves early. The entire yard was a crunchy brown carpet. Right now Lizzie had her back to him, intent on her task. Every few minutes she paused, scooped up a handful of nuts, and tossed them into a wash bucket.

Normally Tommy would have called a greeting to her and kept going—after all, he and Lizzie had seen each other almost every day of their seventeen years. Today, though, the sight of her reminded him of something. He jogged toward her, stopping to pick up a couple of pecans from the cleared area behind her. "You missed some," he called.

Lizzie turned to look at him. "You up already? It's only eleven."

"I don't sleep till noon *every* Saturday." The two pecans in his hand cracked as he squeezed them together, rotated them, and squeezed again. "Besides, I have a social engagement."

Lizzie had already resumed her raking. "Let me guess. You're meeting Goofy Rufie at the fair."

Tommy frowned. It annoyed him a little that his two closest friends didn't care much for each other, but what annoyed him more was that Lizzie always seemed able to read his mind.

"What I came over here for," he said, picking out chunks of pecan, "was to ask you something."

"Well, ask me then."

"It's about the concert tonight."

That got her attention. Very slowly, she turned to him. A tiny half-smile was on her lips, and her eyes... Her eyes looked different, somehow.

Tommy watched her a moment, puzzled, then gulped the last of his pecan and dusted his palms together. "What I was wondering was, I need somebody to watch my little brother tonight while I go. My folks'll be out, and I said I'd stay with him, but now that I'll be gone too, well—"

He stopped in midsentence. Lizzie's face had changed again. Whatever it was that had shone in her eyes for an instant was gone now. Her half-smile was still in place, but now it seemed frozen, and forced.

"Sure, I'll watch Petey for you," she said. "Just send him over when you leave."

She resumed her work. Tommy studied her back, wondering what was wrong. He tried thanking her but she didn't respond, and after a minute of stony silence he turned and left.

"Why is it," Tommy asked, "that you and Lizzie don't like each other?"

Rufus Landers took a bite of candied apple and wiped his mouth on the sleeve of his sweatshirt. "I like her okay," he said, chewing. "She just thinks she's smarter than me, is all."

"She is smarter than you." The two of them were strolling the midway, just inside the entrance to the fair. Their only stop so far had been at a snack stand, where Rufus had wolfed down two chili dogs and bought his apple. Tommy had declined. He was saving his funds for tonight. "She sure was in a funky mood today," he said.

"Girls are like that," Rufus said wisely, glancing around at the rides. "Wanta try the Scrambler or the Spin–and–Whirl?"

But Tommy wasn't listening. The wild euphoria he'd experienced earlier had fizzled, and he felt a little odd. He couldn't seem to get his mind off Lizzie Kelso.

"She seemed okay at first," he said.

Rufus pried a piece of candy from between his teeth. "At first?"

"Yeah, when I told her I was going to the concert tonight she acted fine, like she was pleased about it, you know? Then, when I asked her to keep an eye on Petey for me—"

"Wait a minute. You told Lizzie you were going to the concert...and then asked her to babysit for you?"

"Yeah, I guess. What's wrong with that?"

Rufus snorted. "What's wrong is, Lizzie Kelso's had her eye on you lately. Didn't you know that?"

Tommy stopped walking so suddenly a man behind him almost ran into him. "What?"

"She likes you," Rufus said. "It's beyond me why she does, but she does."

Tommy could only stare. "But Lizzie's just a friend."

"She used to be a friend. She grew up. Which is more'n I can say about *some* people I know." Rufus lobbed his apple core in the general direction of a trashcan twenty feet away. "And in case you haven't noticed, Lizzie's no ugly duckling anymore."

"I didn't say she was. She's just—"

"She's no Yvette McKenna," Rufus finished.

"That's right. She's not." Tommy pondered that a moment. "Yvette *looks* like an Yvette, know what I mean? Lizzie looks...well, she looks like a Lizzie."

After a pause, Rufus said, "The problem is, Yvette *acts* like an Yvette."

"What do you mean?"

Rufus shook his head. "Good grief. And you think *I'm* dumb." He turned and focused on the rides. "Come on, dipweed. Let's do what we came here to do."

Ten minutes later they climbed out of their ride seats and stumbled through the exit chute into the midway. The ground beneath his feet, Tommy noticed, didn't seem to want to stay still.

"I think that thing goes faster'n it used to," Rufus said. Now, from a safe distance, the Spin-and-Whirl looked like a bunch of oversized teacups sitting on a warped saucer. "You're just a bigger pansy now." Tommy studied his friend's chalk-white face. "Sure you're okay?"

"I will be in a minute," Rufus murmured, and took off in the direction of the restrooms, holding his stomach with both hands. "Don't wait up for me, Honey," he called over his shoulder.

Grinning to himself, Tommy continued down the midway. This *was* fun, he decided. The too loud music, the hordes of happy people, the autumn chill, the smell of machinery and sawdust and popcorn...

Then he thought again of Lizzie, home working in her yard. Little Lizzie Kelso, the girl he'd known all his life, the girl he loved like a sister.

Was it true what he'd just heard? Could she have other feelings—different feelings—for him?

Tommy sighed. This kind of thinking made his head hurt. Of course Lizzie wasn't in love with him, any more than *he* was in love with *her*. They were friends. That's all.

But now and then, he thought ... now and then, when she crinkles her eyes a certain way—

A piercing scream snapped him back to reality. He spun around expecting to see a body falling from the Ferris wheel, but the scream had come from a middle–aged woman in a pink jogging suit. Her husband had just won her a stuffed bear.

Feeling glum, Tommy wandered over to one of the other booths, where he watched a smug-looking college kid showing his date how to pitch a softball at milk bottles. The date, tall and tan and blond, reminded Tommy of Yvette McKenna. His spirits lifted.

One o'clock, he thought. Thirty more minutes.

He could hardly wait.

And the great thing was, he knew she was going to say yes. The thought was both scary and thrilling. How could he possibly have been concerned about plain old Lizzie Kelso, when the famous and delectable Yvette McKenna was practically within his grasp?

And, wonder of wonders, it had come about because of two very expensive, very scarce tickets to a rock concert.

For the hundredth time today Tommy reached behind him to pat the pocket that held the wallet that held the tickets, and thanked his lucky stars that his cousin Edward had been obliging enough to come down with the creepy crud now rather than last month, or last week—

Tommy froze.

He felt no comforting bulge in his hip pocket.

Where was his wallet?

Tommy searched his other pockets. Nothing there. He turned in a circle, looking around, his mind replaying his latest movements and actions. Whatever had happened, it had happened within the past fifteen minutes or so. He knew that, because he remembered taking out his wallet to pay for admission to the Spin–and–Whirl.

He blinked.

The Spin–and–Whirl, its wild, jerking motion had thrown both him and Rufus around like ragdolls, their bottoms slipping and sliding on the metal seats as they hung on for dear life.

If his wallet had come out of his pocket—and it had—then it had come out during the ride.

He took off at a dead run, dodging his way back through the crowds.

When he arrived at the Spin–and–Whirl, red–faced and puffing, he felt a surge of hope: The place was deserted, the machinery silent. No one even stood in line. The big teacup looking cars sat empty in the noonday sun.

With barely a pause Tommy dashed along the railing to the ticket booth. The ride operator was nowhere to be seen. A hand–lettered sign said BACK IN 10 MINUTES.

Tommy felt sick. He had to find that wallet. Not only did it contain his two sacred tickets, it also held his emergency funds. Thirty–eight hard-earned dollars.

Still no sign of the ride attendant. For a moment Tommy considered climbing over the railing and searching each car, but he knew that wouldn't work. His wallet had surely been found by now, and probably by the grungy–looking operator he'd seen here earlier.

But he had to try. He was about to step over the railing when a voice stopped him. Tommy's head snapped around so fast it made his neck hurt.

The man who'd spoken, the operator Tommy had seen earlier, was leaning against the sign on the Spin–and–Whirl's ticket booth, both hands stuffed into the pockets of baggy, grease–stained jeans. Topping off the outfit were a ragged flannel shirt, a baseball cap, scuffed cowboy boots, and a gray beard. Long hair spilled from beneath his cap, and his eyes were bloodshot. Several teeth were missing. Everything about him, even his clothes, looked tired.

"I said what do you want? I'm on break."

Tommy's heart sank. This guy was no Good Samaritan. He looked more like an axe–murderer. And since the chances were about a hundred percent that he was the proud new owner of Tommy's wallet, the chances were about zero that Tommy would ever see it again.

But what did he have to lose?

"I think I lost my wallet, in one of your cars," Tommy said, his voice trembling. "My name's inside it. Thomas Bridges."

As Tommy watched, the man removed a pack of cigarettes from his pocket, shook one out, and lit it with a battered lighter. He exhaled a plume of blue smoke that hung there like a fog in the still air. Squinting at Tommy through the cloud, he said, around the cigarette, "You asking if I found it?"

This is crazy, Tommy thought. He blew out a sigh. "No. I guess not. I'm sorry to have bothered—"

"Stay there," the man growled. He turned, opened a gate in the railing, and limped to a small metal shed that crouched like a puppy amid the giant motors and pulleys. A minute later he reappeared, stepping over cables as thick as fire hoses, and held out his right hand. "Look familiar?"

Tommy almost fainted with relief. He opened the wallet. There it was: money, tickets, even the bent stick of Doublemint.

"It's all there. Count it, if you want to."

Tommy swallowed. "I ... can't believe it."

The man chuckled. "I couldn't either. When I made my walk–through, it was laying right there on the seat of Number Four—"

"No, that's not what I meant," Tommy said, and immediately wished he hadn't.

The words seemed to echo in the quiet.

"I know what you meant," the attendant said. As Tommy's face reddened the man rested his forearms on top of the railing and stared Tommy in the eye.

"I'm not offended," the man said. "But there's something you need to remember, Thomas Bridges. Appearances can be ... well ..."

"Deceiving."

"Exactly." He pointed his cigarette like a finger. "You see that bunch over there?"

A ripple of laughter floated over from the other side of the midway. A group of businessmen with suspenders and silk ties and thousand-dollar loafers were trying to toss plastic rings over little revolving pegs without mussing their styled hairdos.

"Be glad those guys weren't the ones found your wallet."

Tommy stared at the man a moment. They both smiled at the same time.

"You're right," Tommy said, the tension gone. A thought occurred to him. "Is there anything"—he shrugged—"anything I can do for you? In return?"

The ride attendant seemed to think that over. Finally he said, "My girlfriend tells me I smoke too much. Maybe my jaws need some exercise."

Tommy frowned then understood. Grinning, he opened his wallet, took out the stick of gum, and handed it over.

"Good trade," the man said.

They shook hands, and Tommy left. Only once did he glance back, and when he did the man was still leaning on the railing, holding his lighter to another cigarette.

Tommy strolled around awhile, adrift in his thoughts. He found Rufus sitting on a bench, staring up at a poster for one of the sideshows. On the sign was a drawing of a scaly long–snouted monster in ladies' clothing and a woolly, hunchbacked giant. FREAKS OF NATURE, the sign said. ALLIGATOR WOMAN AND THE MISSING LINK. Rufus pointed to the sign and said, "Looks like they found your real parents."

"You're lucky, Rufie," Tommy said, plopping down beside him. "I was taught not to hit sick people."

"I've recovered. I look sick to you?"

"Just ugly mostly," Tommy bent down and re–laced his sneakers. "Want to ride something else? Or how about another chili dog?"

"Very funny. I figured you'd still be mulling over your love life."

Tommy thought a moment. "Let's just say I've made some decisions."

"What you better make is a phone call," Rufus said. "Its two minutes till one."

Tommy checked his watch and immediately felt better. "I believe I will." He rose to his feet. "Be a good boy while I'm gone," he added, "and don't talk to any strangers."

Still rubbing his stomach, Rufus watched his friend walk away. "Tell Yvette I'm free next weekend," he called.

Tommy found a pay phone on the wall of a hotdog stand. Nearby, a bunch of kids in bumper cars were bashing their brains out to the tune of "The William Tell Overture." It was 1:01.

He lifted the receiver and hesitated. Now that the time had come, his hand was trembling. Tommy dropped his coins into the phone, took out his wallet, and studied the two concert tickets.

Two little pieces of colored cardboard–they now seemed more important than ever.

He drew a shaky breath and punched in the numbers. His mouth was as dry as sandpaper when he heard her pick up the phone.

"Lizzie?" he said. "It's Tommy ..."

Testimony of Crystal L. Flowers

by Brenda Gable

October 28, 1950

I'd already finished my bath and gotten my pajamas on when I heard someone knocking at the door. It wasn't loud like when Daddy forgets his house keys. It was quieter, like a bird pecking on a tree. Momma answered 'cause I wasn't allowed to after dark and Daddy was working late. I was peeking through the banister to see who it was when Momma let Sally in.

Sally's black cheeks were shiny under the hall chandelier. I could tell she'd been crying. Her hands were twisting around a ratty white handkerchief. Another red handkerchief was tied around her fuzzy hair. Her blouse and skirt were worn but clean. Momma always says even if you don't have much, you need to take care of what you do have. I guess Sally says that too.

"Why Sally, what on earth is wrong?" I heard Momma say. She was as surprised as I was to see Sally this late at night. You see, Sally and Momma aren't friends. She lives down the hill in the old sharecropper house with her husband and kids. Sometimes she comes up and cleans and cooks for Daddy and me when Momma has her spells. Momma started having spells last month after Daddy rushed her to the hospital.

Anyway, Sally sniffed and wiped her tears away with the back of her hand and said, "I have to ask you a favor. I know it's not proper, but I have to know."

"Why, of course. What is it?" Momma asked, waving her hand to invite her in. Normally, people of color come to the back door. But I could see Sally was real upset and so did Momma. Sally spied me upstairs through the railings and stepped back. "Outside. The child doesn't need to know."

Momma looked over her shoulder at me and gave me a look that told me I had best get my fanny back in bed. I didn't, of course. As soon as Momma shut the door behind her, I raced down the stairs to listen to them talk on the veranda. Through the front window I could see them standing under the porch light Momma always left on for Daddy.

"He has another woman. I just know it. He's been late coming home four times this week and three times last week. He tells me he's working late but his paycheck isn't any bigger. If he was working, then there would be more money."

"What do you want from me?" I heard Momma ask right snippy like.

"I don't have a car. I want you to drive me by her house. I just want to see for myself that he's lying to me. A woman needs to know these things for herself."

Momma's chest heaved up once like she was taking in a deep breath of air. She rubbed her eyebrows like she sometimes does when she's upset. "Ok. Let me get coats for me and Crystal."

I turned and raced up the stairs while Momma opened the door to let Sally come in.

"Crystal," she shouted up the stairs. "Get some shoes on. We're going to take Sally for a little ride."

I sat in the back of the big Town Car and listened while Sally gave Momma instructions to a part of town where I'd never been before. The houses were much smaller than ours. There were no sidewalks and not all the street lamps worked. What in the world were we doing here? We never came to the other side of the tracks.

"Stop here," Sally ordered. She got all stiff like and then slumped over. Momma reached over and took her hand. "I'm sorry, Sally."

This high pitched noise came out of Sally's throat. Momma pulled Sally to her chest and rubbed her back while Sally let out the biggest loudest sobs I ever did hear.

We sat there for awhile. I just looked out the window at the rundown house where Mr. Tom's car was parked, and wondered who lived there and why was he there instead of at home with Sally.

Sally went on so long I thought she was gonna flood the car with her tears, then she finally sat up and apologized. "I'm sorry I made you come out. But I had to know."

Momma held onto Sally's hand. "What are you going to do?" Momma asked, this time real nice like.

"I don't know. I ain't got no education. I got pregnant when I was fourteen the first time and he's plowed me with seed every year after that. I have no place to go, no money, no car. My sister moved to Chicago. Maybe I could go stay with her and get a job in the garment business. I should leave the kids with him. It would serve him right."

Momma made shushing noises like when I've scraped my knee. "You know a mother can never leave her children, no matter what."

Sally just slumped some more.

Momma started the car and we pulled away. Sally was shaking real hard like she was cold. "I can't believe he's doing this. He can't afford to feed the mouths he's got and there he goes making more."

It was real quiet in the car going home. I guess there wasn't much to talk about being as they weren't good friends. Momma stopped for a traffic light. Her finger was tapping on the steering wheel while she waited for it to turn green. She looked out the side window and I heard her suck in her breath. Something had scared her. Me and Sally both twisted our necks to see what it was.

Across the street, where she was staring, was a two story house like ours. Lights were on upstairs in one of the bedrooms. A man stood behind the shade and stretched his arms, just like Daddy does. That didn't mean anything to me at the time. Then I saw what got Momma so upset. Daddy's car was parked to the side of the building. Just as bold as brass, his big Cadillac sat under a big ol' oak tree.

I saw Momma turn her face to Sally. It was right sick looking. It was Sally's turn to hold Momma's hand. She didn't say anything. Guess there wasn't much to say. Daddy was visiting like Mr. Tom was and Momma didn't get invited. I leaned back against the leather upholstery. I figured she was going to have another one of her spells when we got home.

Nobody spoke all the way back cause both of them were crying. Shoot, I'd never let someone make me cry because they didn't want me to come to their stupid party. I'd have my own party.

Anyway, when Momma let Sally out at the bottom of the hill, Sally leaned inside the car and said, "Don't do anything foolish, Miz Flowers. You got too much to lose."

Momma took my coat and shooed me on up to bed. Before I fell asleep, I heard her opening drawers in Daddy's room. I guess she finally found what she was looking for 'cause she went back downstairs. I suppose she was gonna wait up for Daddy to ask about the party.

Momma's screaming woke me up. I stuck my head into the hall to see what was going on. She was standing at the top of the stairs. Both hands were wrapped around a gun. She could hardly hold it up 'cause her hands were shaking so bad.

I stepped out into the hall to see better and saw Daddy down below in the foyer at the foot of the stairs where they fan out bigger and come around real pretty like in the movies. Momma was pointing the gun at him. He was holding his hands up to her like he was begging.

"Elizabeth, I swear I was at work," he said. His face was white and covered in sweat. His shirt was sweaty too, under the armpits.

"I saw your car. I know the tag number." Her voice went up even louder. It hurt my ears. I put my hands over them but I could still hear her. "Don't lie to me. You were with your whore."

"No. No. Baby, I was helping Carole Ann with her plumbing. She had a leaky pipe and it was flooding the basement."

He was smiling at Momma as he took the first step. "Put the gun down, Baby. Put the gun down like a good girl."

"Liar!" she screamed so loud I'm surprised it didn't wake the whole county. Her head shook so hard her hair pins went flying everywhere. "You were upstairs in the bedroom. I saw your shadow." Daddy's smile froze along with his feet.

Momma wiped the snot from her nose with one hand. The gun was so heavy she almost dropped it but she caught it and held it up with both hands. "Plumbing," she sniffed. "You were helping her with her plumbing." She laughed real funny like. "Is that the best you can come up with?"

She sat down on the staircase as if she were too tired to stand and laid the gun in her lap. Daddy came up another couple of steps.

"Baby. Elizabeth. Honey, she doesn't mean anything to me. She was just a mistake, just a fling. You mean the world to me. I love *you*."

Momma picked the gun back up and waved it at him. "How long? How long have you been sleeping with that slut?"

Daddy's jaw got real tight, just like it does sometimes when he reads the business section of the newspaper. "Three months." The words came out as a whisper. He cleared his throat and then spoke up a little louder. "The first time was three months ago."

Momma sniffed and swallowed. Her shoulders sagged and her head rolled back. "She's the one who gave it to you." She said it like a statement, not a question. I know 'cause we're studying sentence structure in class and next week we're gonna start diagramming them.

Momma spoke real quiet, like she was whispering to herself. "She gave it to you. You gave it to me. And it killed my baby."

Daddy got a real worried look on his face. "Sweetheart, I know I did wrong. I paid for that mistake. I swear to God, I'm sorry you miscarried. I didn't know she was infected."

"Shut up!" Momma leapt to her feet and waved the gun. "You went back to her. You went back to the whore who killed my baby."

What baby? I thought. Nobody told me anything about any baby. Did she have a baby in her belly and Carole Ann killed it? How did Carole Ann get it out? I wanted to hear more about the baby so I tiptoed closer.

"Baby doll, a man has needs. You cut me off. What was I to do?"

I guess he saw me move because his face got even paler. "Oh, Jesus," he whispered. He looked over Momma's shoulder and talked to me. "Crystal Lynn, go back to bed, Princess. Your momma and I are just having a little argument."

Momma turned to face me. I'd never seen her look like that before. Her make–up was all runny down her face in black streaks. Her lipstick was on crooked too. Snot and tears were all over her face. Her hair had fallen down in her face and her eyes were all wild-like. You know, with the whites all around them. She didn't even look like my momma. That was the first time I got real scared. Momma was having a spell and it was a bad one.

I had heard her and Granny talk about this woman down in Augusta that killed her husband for being a phil–an–der–er. Killed him right dead as a doornail. I guess Daddy was one too. I knew right then and there I had to get the gun away from her or I'd lose my Daddy.

"Momma, come tuck me into bed," I asked her. She just looked at me kinda funny. Daddy came up some more steps real slow while Momma just stared at me like she didn't know how I got there.

"Read me a story, Momma." I held my hand out to her. She looked at my hand and then at the gun in hers.

"For God's sake, put the gun down, Elizabeth," Daddy spoke up louder so she could hear him over her crying. "You don't want to lose another child." He snuck up some more steps. Sweat was just a pouring off his face and dripping onto his shirt.

Momma turned and saw Daddy a few feet away from her. She put the gun up to her head. "Stay back," she yelled.

I knew she was going to kill herself instead of Daddy. She tried to pull the trigger, but the gun wouldn't fire. That was the second time I was real scared.

I remembered what she told Sally. "Momma!" I shouted. "A mother never leaves her child, no matter what!"

She looked at me and her face kinda melted. The gun fell first and then Momma just folded down into a pile on the hall runner. Daddy kicked the gun away and yelled at me, "Go get Sally!" Daddy dropped to the floor and pulled Momma into his arms and started rocking her like a baby. Well, he was kinda like a baby too. Tears were just a pouring out of his eyes. He was sobbing, just like Sally did earlier, his chest going up and down real hard. "Run, Crystal. Ya hear me?" he yelled to me. "Now!"

I took off lickety-split barefoot down the dirt road in my PJ's. Sally flew out of the house when I told her what had happened. She told me to stay. But I didn't because I was scared. By the time we got up the stairs, Daddy and Momma were sitting on the edge of her bed. He had his arms wrapped around her talking real soft to her. He'd gotten her face cleaned up and he'd brushed her hair out so she looked more like my momma.

"I was a fool. I'll never stray again. You are my life. You and Crystal mean everything to me. I swear on my mother's grave I'll never hurt you again. Never. We'll get help. We'll get over the baby's death together. We're a family. God help me, we'll stay a family."

Daddy asked Sally to take me home with her, just for the night. I said, "No." Daddy looked at me real angry. And I just said, "We're a family, Daddy." He held his arm out to me and I snuggled in on his other side and we just held each other and cried together. I woke up in my bed the next morning and went to check on Momma. She was sleeping in Daddy's arms like they used to do, before he had to take her to the hospital.

He opened his eyes when he heard me and said, "She's asleep. Go down and get your breakfast. We'll be down later."

I looked for the gun, but couldn't find it. I thought at the time that Daddy put it back up where Momma couldn't get to it. But, Sally musta picked it up off the hall floor when she went home. I figure that's how the bullets they found in Mr. Tom came from my Daddy's gun.

How Deep the Gulf
by Nancy Gotter Gates

They sat on opposite sides of the room. The silence was palpable, like an unseen presence holding them apart, isolating them in their respective corners. Outside beneath a leaden sky, the Gulf of Mexico was as sleek and gray as a sheet of steel. In their yard the foliage lay stricken from a summer-long drought. The parched grass had long since turned to straw, and the flowers had succumbed with just a flash of crimson or gold among the withered stalks as a reminder of spring's promise.

But the scene outside was beyond their notice, absorbed as they were in their own thoughts. Ellen sat in the rocker that had been her mother's, its faded velvet upholstery replaced by a riot of needlepoint blooms of her own creation. She always felt a sense of peace when she fitted her angular body into its Victorian curves. But today not even the rocker could soothe her. She held her knitting needles tightly, counting off the stitches—knit three, purl one, yarn over—repeating it like a mantra to force out the other thoughts.

Harold sat across from her in his reclining chair that to her had always looked so out of place in her careful collection of family heirlooms, its bulky shape dominating the room like an ungainly pelican squatting in the midst of a covey of delicate sandpipers. But for many years his painful back had demanded the comfort of it. She wondered now why it had annoyed her so all this time. What difference did it make in the overall scheme of things?

He was reading the *Wall Street Journal*, his daily habit. She knew how upset he had been lately as the market had dropped steadily, and the pinched look on his face told her that today's financial news was no better. Was it some masochistic tendency that made him persist in following it? Then she chided herself for doubting his motives. Of course he had to know the market's fluctuations to deal with his investments wisely.

"If anything happens to me," he said repeatedly, "you will be taken care of." His solicitude both warmed and alarmed her.

She looked at her watch and her pulse quickened. She knew that the doctor's office would be emptying now, and he would begin to make his phone calls, the ones to his patients about the results of their tests. She could feel her muscles tighten, the tingling of the nerves along her arms and back, the slight dizziness that always accompanied her fear.

The grandfather clock in the foyer chimed slowly, mournfully. As if it were an echo the phone began to ring. Ellen rose hesitantly and walked toward the sound, its insistent ring pulling her along like a reluctant fish on a hook.

The voice that answered her quavering "Hello" was bold, even ominous, at least to her precarious state of mind.

"This is Doctor Phillips. May I speak to Harold please?"

"It's the doctor," she said holding out the receiver to him.

Harold rose painfully from his chair and walked toward her, refusing to engage her eyes with his.

"This is Harold Gaynor."

A long silence followed while he listened intently, his face a mask that showed neither relief nor despair. Finally he asked, "You're quite sure of that, doctor?" Another brief silence and he thanked him and hung up.

Ellen pressed her hands together to steady them in a prayer-like gesture. "Well?"

"He says the tests are negative, that I'm okay."

"Oh, thank God!" She embraced him tightly, clasping him about the neck as if to assure herself he would always be there. They remained this way for several seconds, Ellen holding him, Harold standing stone-like, not reacting. Finally he pried her arms loose and returned them to her sides. "I don't believe him," he said at last, his voice hollow with the emptiness of one who has given up all hope.

"What do you mean?" She was sure she had misunderstood him.

"I said I don't believe him. I'm going to die. I know it."
His tone was so steady, so matter-of-fact he could have
been discussing the weather.

Ellen was numb. They had been waiting days for the
results of the test, taut with fear, so caught up in the wild
imaginings that accompany the possibility of terminal
illness it was if they were living on a plane apart from their
normal day–to–day existence. While their bodies
participated in the daily routines their minds were
somewhere else, suspended in a limbo of dark and
alarming possibilities.

When she heard the results were negative, a flood of
emotion swept over her, washing away the terrible
thoughts that had dominated not only her waking hours
but her dreams as well. She was so relieved. Her mind
simply could not make sense of what Harold was saying.

She looked at him bewildered. "What are you talking
about? Didn't he say you were okay? Are you keeping
something from me?"

"I told you exactly what he said. The tests were negative
and I've nothing to worry about." He walked over to his
recliner and sat down wearily. "The point is," he continued,
"I don't believe him."

"You think he's lying?" Ellen's knees felt wobbly and
she sank into her rocker.

"Maybe they gave me the wrong tests or they didn't
interpret them right. I just know something terrible is
wrong with me. Nobody can tell me otherwise."

"Harold, you've got to be wrong. Dr. Phillips is a good
doctor. I'm sure he checked every possibility."

"I've got no faith in the medical profession. All they're
interested in is our money."

Ellen's temples throbbed. She knew what prompted
Harold's bitterness and skepticism. It happened years ago.
Ellen had managed in time to deal with it, to accept it as
one of life's tragedies to be confronted and overcome. But
Harold never let go of the sorrow.

"I know you're thinking about Bonnie," she said.
Although she had worked through her grief long ago, the
mention of her name always triggered a painful twinge she
could put no name to. It rendered her momentarily silent.
"You can't stay bitter forever over that."

"The hell I can't."

"Please, Harold, let's not go over that now." She had never been able to convince him that the doctors had tried their best to save their baby. The fact she could never conceive again had riveted the idea into his mind and soul beyond any hope of changing it. "I know it's been a terrible week and believe me, I've imagined all sorts of things too. But you've got to let it go now. You're going to be fine; I'm positive of it."

He looked at her with such bitterness it took her breath away. "You're probably part of it. I'll bet you and the doc cooked all this up for my benefit. He must have told you the truth earlier, and you both decided to lie to me. Well, you're not going to get away with it."

Ellen, alarmed, went over beside Harold's chair, stooped down beside it so she could capture his gaze squarely and took his hands.

"I swear to you that I have not spoken to him. What he says is the truth and you must believe him. You are not ill, Harold; you are perfectly okay. For both our sakes, you must believe that."

He ignored her totally, shutting her out of his cocoon of misery that he had spun so carefully about him. She realized now that he had been creating it for years undetected by her, spinning the first strong invisible threads when Bonnie died so many years ago. She always had known of his mistrust of the medical profession, and he seemed eager to label each new twinge or spasm as symptom of some obscure and alarming ailment. But since his mother had been a hypochondriac on a rather grand scale, Ellen shrugged it off as a mildly irritating habit learned in childhood like poor table manners or not picking up one's socks. She never dreamed it would become an overwhelming obsession. She, too, had been caught up in the fear when the doctor found the menacing shadow on the X–ray, but she was giddy with relief at the good news. Apparently, though, Harold would not accept a reprieve. He could not let go of the idea of his own death.

Ellen tried her best to proceed normally with life as if nothing had happened. Surely Harold would come to his senses in time. She purposely avoided mentioning his health. She reasoned that if he saw she was totally unconcerned, then he would realize there was no basis for his fears.

But while she tried desperately to lead their conversations away from any topic that would trigger his morose self concern, he seemed to be able to twist any subject around to suit his preoccupation.

His delusion did not diminish with time. If anything it grew and flourished in his fertile imagination fed by sleepless nights devoted to conjuring "proofs." He remembered distant relatives who had died of cancer. Past aches, long forgotten, now aligned with other signs as undeniable symptoms.

"Good morning," Ellen would say in all innocence when he appeared at the breakfast table.

"What's good about it?" he'd answer sharply, exhausted from a night of imagining his future course of deterioration.

As the drought continued along the coast and the vegetation continued to wither, Harold's spirit withered too. It seemed to Ellen that the forces of nature were working together to promote his obsession. She prayed silently for a break from the torrid heat that oppressed even her.

At last storm clouds gathered on the horizon, and the forecaster jubilantly predicted they would soon receive some rain. An eerie darkness spread across the sky providing a dramatic backdrop to the jagged bolts of lightning that came at alarmingly frequent intervals. But in spite of all the pyrotechnics, only a few drops of rain fell, not nearly enough to revive the stricken flowers or grass. Soon the sun beat down upon the parched earth again.

"That's always the way," Harold said staring out the window. "Everybody makes lots of promises, but nothing ever comes of them."

"You really can't predict nature," Ellen said, sympathizing with the weathermen.

"That's what I've been trying to tell you. Not even the doctors can do that."

Damn, thought Ellen, whatever I say he's going to interpret to suit his morbid preoccupation.

Ellen had to see Dr. Phillips for her annual checkup the following day. She poured out her story to him and asked for his guidance.

"It's a classic case of a fixed delusion. If you can get him to come in and see me, we should be able to treat it with medication. The sooner the better."

When she returned home, she told Harold the doctor wanted to see him. "He can prescribe something that will make you feel better."

"Hell, no, I won't see him. He just wants to make a few more bucks."

She couldn't convince him to go. Nor did she know what to do now. She had tried every ploy she could think of to shake him out of his delusion but nothing worked. Perhaps if she could understand what drove him to this abandonment of hope, she would know how to handle it. But it was totally beyond her. How could anyone accept death so easily, almost embrace it? She knew all about pain and grief; she'd had plenty of both herself. But she still embraced life as she would a wayward child. It was not always predictable, and it certainly brought her some difficult times, but overall she loved it deeply and unstintingly.

The next afternoon she turned into her street upon returning from grocery shopping and saw her next-door neighbor Betty sitting on Ellen's porch swing in an obvious state of agitation.

She drove hurriedly into the driveway. "What's the matter, Betty?" she called as she scrambled out of her car.

"Oh, my God Ellen, something terrible. Harold's ...," she seemed unable to continue. Finally she pulled herself together. "Harold's ... dead." She embraced Ellen with such fervor she could hardly breathe.

Ellen's mind whirled with questions. Was he sick after all? Did he have a heart attack from worrying about himself? Was he hit by a car?

She released herself from Betty's tight hold. "What happened? How in God's name did it happen?"

Tears ran down Betty's face as she spoke. "Someone in a condo along the beach happened to look out their window and saw him walking straight out into the water. They didn't think too much of it, but he just kept walking until he was in over his head, and he didn't try to swim or float or anything. He just went under and never came up. They called the police right away, but by the time they came and the ambulance, it was too late."

How could he? The silent cry echoed in Ellen's mind. He had everything to live for, and he simply threw it away. He wouldn't even try.

"Where did they take him?" she asked calmly. She wanted to react, she wanted to scream and weep, but she couldn't. She felt only numbness.

"To Saint Anne's, I'll take you there."

When she arrived at the hospital, the doctors took her into a private room and explained to her that he was dead on arrival. The emergency squad had worked on him for nearly forty-five minutes on the beach, but they couldn't revive him. They asked for the name of his physician.

"Dr. Roy Phillips, but I'm sure he's out of town today. He had to attend his daughter's graduation upstate." She remembered how proud he had been talking about his daughter during her examination. She had been surprised at the pang of jealousy she had felt.

They said they would contact him later and asked her to identify the body, although Betty had already done so. 'Next of kin,' they said. Harold looked as though asleep. Maybe he had finally found peace.

Was she up to talking to the police? She said "Yes," and they were as solicitous as they could be. Had he talked of suicide? She said "No," but explained how he was convinced he was dying.

"Did he leave a note?" they asked.

"I don't know. I never got in the house. My neighbor met me outside, and we rushed to the hospital. If I find one, I'll bring it to you."

Betty took her home. "Do you want me to stay with you for awhile?"

"Maybe later, but I need to be alone now."

Ellen entered the empty house reluctantly. In a way she didn't want to find a note because she wasn't sure she could bear what he had to say. On the other hand, if he didn't leave one, she would always live with the fact he didn't even say goodbye.

She didn't have far to look. An envelope bearing her name in his handwriting was propped against the antique clock on the mantel. She thought she detected the faint aroma of his cologne as she opened it. Her hands trembled so violently she had difficulty reading it.

"Dear Ellen, I do love you so, believe me I do. But I can't go on. I'm too much of a coward to face what I know must come. I wish I were strong like you and as optimistic about life. Your strength has gotten me through the other bad times, but it's just not enough now. I'm so sorry I had to do this. Love, Harold."

She sat staring through the picture window at the beach, the beach she had always loved so much. Could she ever walk on it again or gaze upon the surf from her living room window without great pain? It had given her such inner strength and peace before. But now ...

The doorbell rang. Dr. Phillips was standing on the porch when she opened the door, his expression more somber than she had ever seen. *They certainly found him fast,* Ellen thought. "Please come in," she said, gesturing toward the living room, and they sat in matching chairs facing the gulf where the evening sun hovered above the horizon.

"I took the liberty to come by since I was very near here on my way home."

"I appreciate it."

"I have something to tell you. I'm afraid it's bad news."

Ellen looked at him quizzically. Doesn't he think I know about Harold?

"You know those routine blood tests we took during your checkup the other day?"

He doesn't know, she thought. He's not talking about Harold. This is something else.

"Well, I'm afraid they show abnormal white cells. We need to do some more tests as soon as possible so we can begin treatment. I must emphasize the urgency of this."

It took her some seconds to grasp what he was saying before the full impact hit her like a blow to the midsection. It was *she* he was talking about. Not Harold.

"I called you this morning to tell you. Harold answered and said you were out. He insisted I tell him my findings, but he wanted me to tell you personally. He couldn't bring himself to do it. He seemed very upset. Is he all right?"

She didn't answer, but looked out the window instinctively. The sun was setting now amidst a panorama of mauve and amber clouds. It had dipped halfway into the gulf, but as always, for what seemed like seconds, it appeared to hesitate, to flatten out along the edge of the horizon as though the sea refused to accept it.

Grandpa and the Hoop Snakes
by Edward Hartman

Well, Son, it was like this. About sixty years ago, when I was about your age, we was a havin' a big problem with the hoop snakes on the hillside. Ever' day or two my pa sent me up on there to fill my bag with pine lighter knots 'cause they make it easy to start a fire in that big ol' wood stove he bought. I would always take my dog Scout with me to protect me from those darn hoop snakes. Hoop snakes won't ever bother you if you have a dog along.

Well, one day, as luck would have it, I had to go gather more lighter knots, an' I had loaned Scout to my friend down the holler fer rabbit huntin'. I tried ever' excuse I knew to get out of that chore jes' for that day. Nothin' worked on Pa.

"Go," he said, "or we won't be able to start no fire tomorrow."

Well, I didn't have no choice. I had to go, hoop snakes or no. Well, I tell you I was mighty scared. Those hoop snakes is all fired dangerous and would attack with no warnin' at all. They should'a had rattles like a decent rattlesnake. No, Sir, those hoop snakes is as sneaky as a egg–suckin' dog. No warnin' at all. Well, there I was up on that hillside, the most dangerous place I could ever' be. Jes' by luck, I happened to look up jes' in time to see one of those devil hoop snakes a comin' right after me.

Well now, let me tell you what a hoop snake looks like. They is at least eight foot long and have two big horns on top o' their head an' they is flame red. The thing that makes them so all fired dangerous is they can grab their tail in their mouth and form a perfect loop. Then down the hill they would come a rollin' jes' like a wheel. If one hit you, those horns would go square into your back, dump their p'ison in you an' kill you dead right on the spot.

Well, here comes that hoop snake a rollin' right after me. The farther he rolled the faster he got. Well, now, I tell you, Son, I was a mighty fast runner myself in those days. So down the hill I run, lookin' over my shoulder ever' so often to check on that hoop snake. No matter how fast I run, that hoop snake kept right on a gainin' on me. I figured that if I didn't think of somethin' mighty quick, I was a goner fer sure. Then I thought of a way to get that critter off my tail.

I let that ol' hoop snake get real close to me, an' then I jumped behind a big white oak tree. Well, that hoop snake was a goin' so fast he couldn't make that turn. An' he buried his horns right smack dab in the middle of that oak tree. Try as he might, he couldn't break loose. I gathered me up a big stick an' let him have it.

When I tol' Pa how I done it, he had me a goin' up on that hillside ever' day until I got rid of all those hoop snakes. Now if you don't believe it, you can go up on that hillside an' see hoop snakes' skeletons a hangin' from ever' white oak tree. And the best thing is I become the fastest runner in my school.

Sighted Brother
by Deborah J Ledford

Long shadows from a half-moon's light cut across the path of galloping mustangs on the wallpaper of the ten year old, twin boys' bedroom. Along one wall, row after row of books stood on bowing shelves. The opposite wall featured baseball banners.

"Talk to me, Joe," Willie said.

"I've talked to you all day. Hush up," Joe said; thinking of the picture he had begun to draw of the graveyard not far from their home, heavy with kudzu clinging to ancient stone walls.

"I'm worried," Willie said.

"It'll be okay. Dad said you prob'ly just need glasses."

Joe thought of the game of catch they had played two weeks ago—the *thud* as the baseball hit Willie between the eyes. Willie's screams. Willie's blood. Joe shuddered.

"What'cha thinkin', Joe?"

Joe's eyes shot open. "Dang it, go to sleep."

"Can't," Willie rustled in his bed across the room. "Come on. What'cha thinkin'?"

Joe knew his brother would keep pestering him until he answered, so he asked, "What're *you* thinkin'?"

"Thinkin' about wonderin' what you're thinkin' about." Willie giggled.

Joe swung to meet his brother's gaze. Darkness stared back. "You're always wonderin' about me, aren't you?"

"Sure. You're my best friend."

"We're brothers. Not friends."

Willie's bed creaked. "Both. We're both. Unless you don't wanna be."

"What? Your brother or your friend?"

"Don't you wanna be both?"

Joe rolled his eyes. "All right, we're both. Now quit."

"Night, Joe."

Joe clenched his teeth. "No more gabbin'."

"'Kay," Willie whispered.

* * *

The next morning at dawn, the crisp air thick with fog, Willie's glum parents ushered him into the eight year old '62 Buick Electra, and drove into the Clarksdale, Mississippi mist.

Their grandparents stayed with Joe throughout the day. His grandmother crocheted a single chain stitch Joe swore could circle the house twenty times, while his grandfather paced the living room floor, flicking his gaze back and forth to the window.

His grandparents said the empty words of encouragement, "Everything will be all right," so many times that Joe stalked off to his shared bedroom. He took up his baseball mitt that smelled of leather and saddle soap and tossed the ball into the well-formed web over and over, scanning the books above Willie's bed.

Darkness had fallen by the time Joe heard his parents' car. Only two doors slammed shut. His mother shouted for Willie to come back. Joe drew back the curtain as his father said, "Let him go. He can't get far." His scared, tired voice sounded older than Joe's grandfather's.

Joe waited for his brother, but an hour later, he remained alone. He crept down the creaking stairs and dropped to the bottom step, seeing his mother standing in the kitchen.

She wept into the phone. "They call it Macular Degeneration. It's an old man's disease. He's going blind, Myra." Sobs jerked her body. Clutching the handset, she slid down the wall and crumpled into a tight ball.

Hours later, Joe heard Willie's fingertips skim the wall along the hallway to their room.

"Where you been?" Joe whispered.

Willie didn't answer. By moonlight, he stripped down to his boxers and T–shirt and settled into his bed. After a long time, he finally spoke. "Turns out, I don't need glasses."

Joe slid from his worn sheets to the matching ones across the room and nudged in next to his brother. His grandparents' hollow words rang in his ears. "Don't fret, Willie. Everything will be all right."

Willie sniffled, reaching for Joe's hand.

* * *

One day found them riding to the post office on a crowded city bus. Cradling a Christmas package wrapped in butcher paper, Willie asked, "What's it look like out there, Joe? Is it beautiful?"

"Beautiful?" Joe rolled his eyes. "You sound like a girl. It's the same old countryside it's always been, kudzu chokin' the life outta everything. Hasn't changed a bit since ..." Joe trained his eyes on the worn floor. "It looks the same."

"Some things are beautiful."

"Nothin's beautiful around here, believe me."

"Mama's beautiful," Willie said, a proud grin on his lips.

"Well, you haven't seen her too good lately."

Willie turned his unfocused gaze on Joe. "What's wrong with her?"

"She just worries."

"About me."

"No, not about you," Joe snapped. "It's not always about you." Passengers turned and looked at them, so he lowered his tone. "It's that damned mill. It's killin' her."

"Maybe she could find somewhere else to work."

"There's nothin' else in this backward hick town," Joe mumbled.

A little girl continued to stare at Willie. Joe thought the mother would reprimand her, but instead, they both covered their mouths and laughed.

"Mind your own business," Joe yelled. "Why are you teachin' your kid to be so rude?" He gritted his teeth so tight his jaws hurt.

When the bus stopped, he tugged Willie's arm and led him down the steps of the bus. Emerging onto the bustling sidewalk, Willie's voice stuttered, "I'm scared, Joe. Too many people." He crushed the box to his chest.

"Hold on to me. And be careful with Aunt Jessie's present. Mama will have our heads if that thing breaks."

Willie hooked a finger in Joe's belt loop and tucked in close. The box, tinkling with Aunt Jessie's now broken Christmas vase, bumped against Joe's lower back. Shuffling in step, parting the way, the sighted brother led the other to safety.

* * *

One night, Joe sat at the table in the kitchen across from his mother and complained, "People always stare at Willie."

"That's because he's special," she said, awe in her voice, watching Willie sitting in the living room, staring at nothing.

Joe stopped his pencil mid-stroke. "What do you mean?"

"He's a sight to behold," she said, "so smart and sweet."

Joe gawked at her.

His beaming mother wrenched her gaze from Willie to land on Joe. "Not that you aren't, Joey." She attempted to tame his cowlick. "You're always looking after your brother. That makes you special, too."

Joe pushed away from her touch. "I don't wanna be special."

Willie scraped oatmeal from the earthenware bowl with his spoon. "Read it again."

"No." Joe slapped the cognitive theory textbook shut and slid it the length of the table. "I don't understand any of it."

"That's okay. I do. Almost. I think I'm being thrown by the emphasis you're making on certain words. Just read it, you know, meditatively."

"Stop pushin' me."

Willie's fingers crawled along the Formica, his nose inches from the surface. He pulled the text to him and caressed the imitation leather cover. "Ten more minutes."

"I'm stupid, Willie. If I'm gonna read, it'll be somethin' that don't make my brain hurt. Besides, I've got things to do."

Willie smiled. "Like finishing that drawing of Julie you've been working on?"

"Shut up!"

"I know you think about her. I know you, Joe."

Joe snatched the book from Willie's grasp. "You don't know me at all."

Willie kept smiling. "Chapter fourteen."

"You're tryin' to bore me to death. Dang thing don't even have any pictures." Joe flipped to chapter fourteen. "You're never gonna use this stuff in real life, you know."

"I want to be ready for the college entry exam. You know I wouldn't ask for your help if I didn't have to, right?"

Joe nodded.

"You know that, right?"

"I said, okay."

"You didn't say anything. You've got to say it."

Joe leaned in close to Willie and shouted, "Okay. I'm going to read from this piece of crap book now."

Willie turned serious. "You're not stupid. Don't ever say that again."

Willie sat alone at the scuffed desk in their bedroom. Every light ablaze, he held a magnifying glass inches from a textbook.

Joe burst into the room and ripped off his soaked windbreaker. Raking his hair with wet hands, he began a furious pace on the braided rug.

"What's wrong, Joe?"

"She's leavin'."

"Who?"

"Julie Wyzinski. She's goin' away with that prick, McAllister."

Willie straightened up in the chair. "Derrick McAllister? The quarterback?"

Joe glared at Willie. "Yeah, the asshole that shoves you in the lunchroom every day at school."

Willie's shoulders slumped, he massaged his left shoulder.

"He's been accepted at USC. Full scholarship. She's goin' with him."

"To California?"

"She says he'll play ball and go to school." Joe took a girlish stance, one hand on his raised hip, the other limp at the wrist. "While she auditions for the movies. Oh, or TV, she's not particular."

"But, I thought she was your girl."

"Nope. She says we're just friends. After all, we haven't even kissed. Besides, she can't be expected to stay here, that would make her common. She's got talent. Gonna be a star!" Joe kicked the dresser so hard Willie flinched. "Dammit, I should have kissed her. I'm a loser. Her decision was easy."

"She'll be back. People leave here, but they always come back."

"Yeah," Joe mumbled, "when they're in a wooden box."

The letter arrived on their seventeenth birthday. Willie bobbed one foot to the other. "What does it say?"

"It's from Belhaven College." Joe's heart pounded in his ears as he read the letter to himself.

"Joe?"

Joe scrunched the sheet of formal letterhead into a ball and tossed it at Willie's chest. "It says you're goin' away."

"I made it? They accepted me?" He fell to his knees, searching for the letter. "We did it, Joe. You and me."

"I'm not goin' anywhere."

Willie's smile dropped off his face. "What do you mean?"

"It's your name on the letter. Not mine."

"But you're going, too. They know all about me. That I need help. Your help."

"You expect me to lead you around campus while you go to classes I'd never be caught dead in? You think I oughta keep doin' what I've done every day of my miserable life since we were ten? No way, man. It's over." Joe punched the air above his head in victory. "Finally, I'm free from your stupid questions."

"Don't talk like that."

"You think I'll miss it? Miss you?" Joe advanced on Willie. "Miss the hell you've put me in?"

"It's not my fault, Joe."

Joe clenched his fists. "You're right. It's not. It's not even about that." He lowered to his haunches and stared into Willie's eyes. "It's about responsibility. And fact of the matter is, you're mine."

"It'll be all right."

Joe shoved Willie's shoulder. "No, it won't."

"Why are you so mad?"

"Don't you get it? You're all I know how to do. You've been my chore, my job, my life since we were little kids." Joe resumed his pacing. "You know the only way out of this town is by bein' a genius and gettin' a scholarship like you, or maybe as a football hero. I'm only second string on the team, and I sure as hell ain't no genius. So, I guess I'm pretty much screwed."

"There are probably art schools in Jackson. You could..."

"I could what? Hang out with a bunch of pussies? No way."

"But you're good, Joe. Really good."

"How the hell would you know?"

"I know," Willie murmured. "Besides, what will you do if you don't come with me?"

"Stay here. Mom will get me a job at the mill. I'll save up. Buy a hot car. Find a girl to date, now that I won't have you to baby-sit."

"You can't do that."

"What, find a girl?"

"No, work in the mill. You hate that place. You call those people losers. You'll die doing that."

"I don't got no other options. Anyway, the university has a special services department. That's the reason our parents applied for you to go there." He went to Willie and pulled him up to meet him eye to eye. "You don't need me."

"That's not true." Willie's voice lowered. "And you need me."

"What are you talkin' about?" Joe snapped.

A long silence filled the stuffy room.

Finally, Willie answered. "What else have you got?"

Before dawn the next day, Joe rifled through his sleeping father's wallet and took the meager amount of bills. He raided the money his mother hoarded in a hidden flour tin. Stuffed clothes into his father's old Army duffel, scribbled out a note of goodbye, and disappeared into the fog.

He only made it across the Louisiana state line when the money ran out. After finding a job mucking stalls at a horse ranch in Vicksburg, Joe wrote his parents a letter letting them know where he was, that he was fine, but not to expect him home anytime soon.

Eight months later, Joe received his only phone call. Standing in the stable, rake in one hand, phone in the other, his father's voice crackled over the static on the line.

"Joe. I'm callin' about your brother."

"What is it, Dad?"

Silence hung so long Joe thought he had lost the connection.

"I need you to bring his coffin home."

Joe's knees buckled. "What?"

"I can't leave your mama. She's barely holdin' on from grief."

Joe slid down the knotty pine wall. "What happened?"

"His group of kids were crossin' the street, but I guess the woman leadin' 'em lost track of Willie. The truck driver told the authorities all the kids and their canes wavin' around distracted him. Willie fell back from the group. Maybe he stumbled. Nobody knows for sure. The driver never saw him."

Too stunned to speak, Joe could only shake his head.

"Come home, Son."

Joe caught the next train to Jackson, Mississippi. Rolling into the station, he noticed a coffin on a wheeled cart parked at the edge of the landing. A man in black slacks and jacket, his skin dark as the walnut casket, stood beside it waving away a fly with his cap.

Joe ran to the man before the train stopped. Heart pounding, he stared at the coffin. "Excuse me, sir. Is this my brother?" He squeezed his eyes shut, praying the man would say "No."

The man took a sheet of paper from his pocket, "Says this here's William Ronald Cochran."

"What's he doin' out here?" Joe shouted.

"Waitin' on the train to Clarksdale."

"Couldn't you have put him inside?"

"They tole me to stay out here with him." The man gave Joe an easy smile, his teeth white as his shirt. "Don't you worry none. I been keepin' him cump'ny. Name's Marcus."

Joe let out a ragged breath. "He would'a liked that. I'm Joe."

For two hours the men waited, Willie between them, Joe's hand occasionally resting on the lid of the wooden box. By the time the train's whistle announced its arrival, Joe had told Marcus everything about his twin.

Marcus lifted the cart's handle and led it to the last train car. "No passengers at this stop but you. Best hurry on to your seat."

"I'm stayin' with him."

"Oh, no, sir. They won't allow that."

"I'm not leavin' him again."

Marcus flipped the steel bar mounted outside the train car, then yanked out a ramp. He pulled the shaft of the cart as Joe pushed from the back. Settling the wagon inside, Marcus blocked the wheels in place, and gave the casket a pat. "Pleasure meetin' you, Willie."

When Marcus leapt from the train, Joe didn't follow.

"You sure about this, Son? Long ride."

Joe nodded.

"All right, but you best keep the door shut." Marcus shoved the ramp inside, took a whistle from his pocket, and blew it. The train began to roll.

Joe returned Marcus' wave then tugged the door closed. Light shafted through cracks in the planks casting dusty rays on the gleaming casket. Leaning against the rusty wall, Joe rested an arm on the smooth, cool wood and drifted off to the clatter of wheels on rails and the lulling motion.

"What's it look like, Joe?"

Joe's eyes shot open. He looked around the empty car, and then stared at Willie's coffin. Arms out to keep his balance, he crossed to the door and opened it wide. Clutching the doorframe, Joe inhaled deeply. Humid, lush air and the locomotive's soot filled his lungs.

"The pines are covered in kudzu, just like back home." Then Joe looked closer. "Oak trees stand just beyond the tracks, their leaves are bright greenish–yella' like new rye grass. I see bright blue lobelia and cardinal flowers, and somethin' like those little flowers Mom calls white bells." Joe chuckled, returning to his brother. "You'd say it's beautiful."

The years passed and Joe exchanged his drawing pads for a camera. He traveled the world taking photographs and recording commentary, explaining in minute detail everything framed within the snapshots; how hard he had cried after clicking the picture of a fireman carrying a lifeless little girl from a burning building. The stillness of his soul, staring breathless into a pit filled with skeletons in Cambodia. The cacophony of sound and a thousand shades of green in the Amazon rainforests of South America. A courtyard in Calcutta overrun with children returning Mother Theresa's smile.

Joe anticipated every question Willie might have asked. Willie's words, *"What's it look like, Joe?"* would ring in Joe's ears, urging him to describe each photograph precisely as he would have relayed the details to his twin. Because of Willie, Joe channeled stunning images even the sightless could see.

Motorcycle Mama
by Philip L. Levin

Friday, my last day at the clinic, wound to a close. When my husband died I signed up as an aide. After three years of working eight hours a day and going to college at night, I had finally earned my nursing degree. Next week I would start my new job at the hospital. Martin met me in the break room just before closing.

"So I guess I'm never going to get that beer," he said. I had lost a silly bet a couple of weeks before and he'd been bugging me all week about collecting.

"And I guess I'm never going to get that motorcycle ride," I replied.

At twenty-five years old, Martin radiated the pride of his prolonged adolescence when he brought all of the clinic staff out to the parking lot to see his new bike last month. Silly me. I wonder what made a fifty year old nurse say, "I've always wanted to ride one."

He had locked eyes with me. "Then I promise you a ride."

That month passed quickly, and now it looked like neither promise would be fulfilled.

"What are you doing after work tonight?" Martin asked.

"Oh, really now. Don't you think I'm a little old to be a Motorcycle Mama?"

"Never too old. You're in great shape. You said riding a bike has always been one of your dreams."

Raising a child and making a home had always been higher priorities for me than silly things like motorcycles. Then my husband developed cancer, and all thoughts of frivolity became mere daydreams. Like a motorcycle, life sometimes races down unexpected roads.

I smiled. "Would you really want to take an old woman like me out on a bike ride?"

Martin's lips curled at the edges. "For an older lady, you're damn cool. I've always liked working with you. You care about the patients and that shows. Come on, Betty. After work I'll ride home and pick up my extra helmet. You go to your place and change into the thickest jeans you have, a leather jacket if you have it, boots and gloves. I'll pick you up at your apartment."

I hesitated only a moment more. "Hell. Why not? You only live once."

At my apartment I dressed the part, finding my husband's old flight jacket I'd kept in a trunk. I tried some deep knee bends and found I could rise with little effort. When I heard the bike roar up, I hurried to the door.

Martin helped adjust the surprisingly weighty helmet, and tied a bright yellow scarf around my neck. "It'll blow in the wind like a kite tail," he promised. "Now listen. Try to sit straight, which means don't lean when I lean. Hold on tight! Bouncing off the bike at sixty will leave a lot of that skinny butt of yours on the road."

Climbing on behind him, I grasped Martin's waist, feeling the purr of the bike radiate up my thighs. With a roar we shot off down the highway. The wind buffeted the helmet and pulled at my clothes, whipping that yellow scarf with snaps that sang with joy. Mississippi oaks towered overhead, silent witnesses to our transit.

Martin weaved past cars that must have been going seventy. I could hear nothing but my heart pounding, a boom–de–boom of volcanic excitement. My eyes glistened with tears, creating halos around streetlights. Martin paused at the top of a bridge, pointing to a boat heading towards the reds of the fading sunset. We zoomed away with a jolt.

Martin pulled to a stop in the parking lot of a sleazy bar. "Ready for my beer," he announced as he helped me off.

He held the door open as I followed him into the dimly lit, country music blasting tavern. My nose wrinkled at the power of stale beer, thick with cigarette smoke, tinged with sweat and pot. Massive fellows with tattoos battled at the two billiard tables. A couple of wide–ass girls giggled over drinks and cigarettes at the bar. Martin headed to a table in a corner and I sauntered up to the bar to buy our beers. With my wide–legged gait, I felt like a cowgirl. I brought back the two bottles and some tiny napkins. I dabbed ineffectively at the layers of dried rings.

Martin raised his Miller Lite in a salute. "To a happy Motorcycle Mama." We clinked the bottles and took swallows. Cold and wet, the alcohol raced to my brain.

"So you've never ridden a chopper before? What'd you think? Like it?"

My heart still pounded in my chest, my temples, and my crotch. "All I can say is WOW! That's the most fun I've ever had."

Martin's cheeks wrinkled, almost a smirk, and drank down half his beer. "With those long legs of yours, you're a natural biker. You do look great in jeans. I've only seen you in those loose scrubs before this."

I couldn't stop trembling, I felt so giddy. "Is it always this good or will I get jaded after a few times?"

Martin finished his beer and shrugged. "Some people live to ride, especially gals. Rubs them the right way, if you know what I mean."

I blushed, because I did know what he meant.

"Good beer," I said. "Are you having another?"

Martin shook his head. "Not if I'm gonna get you home safely. You up for a second one?"

"No. I'd hate to lose my grip." Two could play at that double entendre game.

A fat–jowled bearded man wandered up to our table and raised an open hand. Martin grasped it with a laugh.

"Hey Bubba," Martin said. "What's cooking?"

"Who's the hot chick?" Bubba replied, leering at me. I kinda liked it.

"Bubba, Betty. Betty, Bubba," Martin said. "Betty works with me at the clinic. Well, she used to. Today was her last day. We're celebrating her new job."

"Hell, I'll drink to that," Bubba said. "I'll get us another round." He turned and started to the bar.

"Hold on," Martin called. Looking at me he asked, "You sure you don't want another one?"

I shook my head. "No more. I'd rather get back on the bike."

"Right-o." Still staring at me he called to Bubba, "Gotta get back on the road. Catch you on the flop."

Martin stood, helped me up, and led me to the door. Moments later we blasted off, racing out of the stratosphere.

Sixty, seventy, eighty, ninety, maybe a hundred miles an hour, we streaked along empty country roads Martin knew well. The stars twinkled in the brilliant black sky. Outlines of trees shot by in shadowy canopies. I held on for dear life, squeezing tight against his back, bouncing over road cracks, flying off little hills.

As a child I loved the roller coasters, the thrill of plummeting down that first steep mountain and rocketing around twists and corners. This motorcycle ride excited me ten times more than those coasters, or downhill skiing, or anything else I had ever done. By the time Martin pulled up to my apartment I could barely catch my breath. Slipping off the back of the bike my legs trembled, refusing to support my weight.

"You going to be okay?" he asked. "You need help?"

I nodded weakly and draped my arm over his shoulders as we climbed the steps and into my place. I collapsed on the couch and watched Martin go to the kitchen.

"Beer or water?" he called out from inside the refrigerator.

I knew I should ask for water. "Beer."

"So, I gather you liked it?" He handed me a cold open bottle and took a swig from his.

I nodded. "I have *got* to get one of those things!"

Martin grinned. "What did you like about riding?"

I felt tears coming to my eyes. "Martin, it wasn't that long ago that I felt that my life was over. Three years ago the man I thought I'd live with forever died in my arms. I found myself with huge debts and an unknown future. Since then I've been working my way back, having to give up the house for this apartment, and going to school at nights. Now I finally feel I'm back on the road.

"But until tonight, I had no flame inside. I lived because I had to. I struggled and studied and cried myself to sleep. Tonight my heart pulsed with fire. We raced like antelopes, a thrill for life I haven't enjoyed in years.

"You know what? I feel like I want to experience all of the wonders I've missed! I want to parachute from airplanes, kayak down the Amazon, make love on the beach. Kiss me!"

Martin's smile faltered. "Excuse me?"

"You heard me. Kiss me!" I stood and went to him, arms open wide.

"Are you sure?"

I looked in his frightened eyes, and turned away. "I'm sorry. For a moment I forgot I'm just a foolish old woman. Please forgive me."

Tears flooded my eyes. I felt his hand on my shoulder turning me to him.

"No, Betty. You're no older than you feel. I'd love to kiss you."

And he did.

Let Me Down Easy
by Denton Loving

I steered her old Dodge pick-up with one hand across gravel back roads toward Saltville. Amanda leaned up against me, our bodies riding the bumps in the road together. I was coming down from the drunk, and our talking, which had been feverish for awhile, had settled into something quiet and calm like the night around us. Except for her telling me where to turn, there was only the noise of the motor and static from the radio as she searched from one station to another.

"Seems like there ain't no good stations anymore," I said.

Her hand paused as we heard Johnny Cash for a second. The station went out as fast as it came, and she finally gave up.

"Don't matter. We'll be there soon." She switched on the CD player, and I recognized the band that had been playing earlier at the Mill, their fiddle noises floating around the truck and into the surrounding hills as if their music belonged out there.

A couple of the guys from the band were driving behind us. My brother Noah was back there somewhere too. It was the middle of the night, but we made a train of headlights through the dark country, on our way to somewhere else where we would try to keep the evening from ending.

Amanda told me to turn left, onto another gravel road. This one sloped uphill before plummeting down in a curve. We passed an ancient farmhouse with a dim light coming from the first floor. The moon above was nearly full, and I could tell the house was in bad shape like most of the others we had passed. Barbed wire fences lined the road. We crossed a cattle bridge and entered a field of tall grass ready to cut for hay. On top of another hillside, I geared into park. Amanda pulled a blanket out from behind the seat as she stretched her legs to the ground.

"Bring that Thermos with you," she said over the other car doors and people's voices. "I stole some of the Mill's secret punch tonight. Ever had any?"

I shook my head no and followed her out into the middle of the field. She spread her blanket on the ground and motioned for me to take my place beside her. We were out in the middle of nowhere, high up on some ridge. It was the kind of night when you look at the stars and think no one else could ever have seen them be so bright. You know it's crazy, but that's how you feel.

"Be careful," Amanda said. She opened the Thermos and held it under my nose for me to get a whiff of its strength. "It's full of fruit. You eat too much of the fruit and you'll go blind crazy." She smiled as she took a sip, careful as she swallowed. Then she flashed a piece of cut-up apple between her teeth, before handing the Thermos back to me.

I wouldn't have been out that night if Noah hadn't forced me. I sat perched at the bar at the Mill, feeling sorry for myself and watching Noah with admiration as he negotiated through the crowd towards Janie and Joy Hopkins.

"Those girls are just plainly the finest pieces of ass in Smyth County," Noah said before moving in their direction.

They were good-looking, but I never could tell them apart. I haven't talked with either of them enough to be impressed by any sort of distinguishing personality traits.

"Girls like that make you reckless," I said.

"Girls like that'll sink you to hell, but you'll have a good time going." He took a long chug from his bottle of Blue Moon. "If you'd come out more often, you'd remember why girls like that are fun. Why don't you come dance? There's two of them and two of us."

"You got me here tonight, but I ain't dancing. Don't push your luck."

"All right, but you mark my words. Move on or rust out."

Noah handed me his empty bottle and left me for the girls. He entered their conversation and made himself the focus of their attention in an instant. He stood between them with his arms wrapped around their shoulders. They all smiled and laughed and waited for the music to start.

Those actions weren't Noah's alone, or at least they didn't used to be. I was half proud of him and half humiliated at him showing me up. *I taught that boy everything he knows,* I told myself. *But I was someone else back then.*

I slammed back the last of my Miller Lite and waited for someone behind the bar to notice I was empty. The Mill was packed though, and the thunk of my empty bottle didn't register in anyone's hearing. It was while I was waiting that I first recognized Amanda. I had known her a long time ago, back when I was that person I used to be. She had worked at a couple of different bars in Abingdon, all places I quit frequenting when I met Michelle. We flirted a lot but it never went any deeper.

Amanda was still a pretty young woman with dark skin and hair and big, brown eyes, not much different from the other girls I had seen that night. She was prettier than a lot of the others, but it wasn't her looks that really set her apart. She smiled so genuinely to everyone. I knew she was having a better time than those she served. Shuffling down the bar from customer to customer, she mixed liquor, filled pitchers and opened bottles in a furious pace.

The band came on stage to begin their first set with the fast rhythm of a guitar, immediately calling people from every side of the building to the big wooden dance floor. I watched the crowd mix together in the center of the room. Some people stayed in the back to give themselves more room to dance, but others pushed their way through, wanting to get close enough to the stage to feel the pulse of the music blast through the speakers. The fiddle player raced his bow back and forth to give a piercing quality to their song. I turned back to the bar, and waited for Amanda to get to me. When she saw me waiting, she winked.

"Been a long time since I've seen you," she said, taking my empty bottle and replacing it with a full one. "Why ain't I ever seen you in here before?"

"I stopped going out when I got married." The bottle met my lips, and I felt the coldness of the beer run down my throat and all through me.

"I didn't take you for an old married man."

"I'm not married anymore. Now I'm just old."

The expression on her face told me she already knew my situation, or maybe there just wasn't much that could surprise her. She looked down and reached under the bar for a fresh, white cloth. With one hand, she wiped down the bar, soaking up other people's spilled beer and the water rings left from cold bottles.

"I'm sorry to hear that," she said, still swabbing down the polished bar top. Then, she looked up, directly at me. "On the other hand, I guess that means you and me are free to have a good time tonight." Her eyes met mine straight on, and I turned, somehow afraid to look straight at her.

Most of the people who had surrounded the bar earlier were out on the dance floor. Amanda went back to pouring drinks and collecting empties. She kept a fresh bottle in my hand while I watched all the couples on the floor. Noah danced with both of the Hopkins girls. He occasionally caught my eye and motioned for me to come out, but I ignored him. After a time, Amanda came around the bar and sat on the empty stool next to me.

"You like the band?" She propped her elbow on the bar, giving away the first indication I had seen all night that she wasn't tireless.

"They're good," I said.

I had never heard them before, but I liked them. I understood full well why Noah liked them. They used a harmonica in most of their songs. Some of it was fast and fun and gave their music a rough edge like my little brother. And some was long vibrating drones, full of melancholy and the kind of sorrow I wanted to wallow in. The big double bass kept the song's steady beat. I could feel every pluck of the strings as if they ran up and down my spine.

"You got plans for later tonight?" she asked.

"I don't have any plans. Period." I turned my body toward her, and my knee bumped into her before I could move it around her. "Sorry," I said.

"I'm not hurt." She smiled. "Stick around until we close, and we can talk more. I think a bunch of us are going out to a place I know afterwards. We'll sing and dance under the stars and go to sleep where we fall."

"I probably won't be much company."

"Why don't you let me decide that for myself?" She leaned into me and looked at me again like she had earlier. I felt her trying to pull me out of myself and into her. I knew at that moment I was supposed to kiss her, but I couldn't. I couldn't kiss Amanda because, even though Michelle had left me, it seemed so wrong. Amanda must have realized I wasn't going to follow through, and finally, she took her hands off me and grabbed the bar.

"Chuck," she called to one of the bartenders. "We need some shots over here." Then she turned back to me. "You gonna do a shot with me?" She smiled, and I knew I hadn't completely blown it with her. Even more so, I knew I wanted another chance to get it right. There was something so open about her when I looked in her brown eyes, something about the way she looked into me when we talked.

I knew Amanda saw my pain, knew I was different than I used to be, but she saw past that too. When Amanda dispensed drinks at the Mill, she wasn't just covering up people's problems with alcohol. She was truly interested in those people. She was the kind of girl who wanted a real answer when she asked how a person was doing.

"What do you want to do?"

"How about an Irish car bomb?"

"That sounds the way I feel, so why not." I tried to smile back at her.

Her eyes studied me again, and for a moment, she looked as if she were the one in pain. "Never mind. No Irish car bombs for you. You need something to get the blood flowing again. How about a Jager bomb? You ever had a Jager bomb?"

I shook my head no and took a drink of Miller.

"I think that's just what we both need to get going tonight," she said. She pulled her hair behind her ear with two fingers.

Chuck handed Amanda a Red Bull, which she opened with a pop and fizzing sound. She split the can between two tall glasses while Chuck twisted the top of the green bottle of Jagermeister. The dark liquid filled two empty shot glasses, and Chuck walked away. It smelled like cough syrup.

"Drop the entire shot glass in the Red Bull and drink both," she said. I followed her, allowing the two liquids to mix together in my mouth. Instead of a medicine taste, the two drinks formed a minty flavor in my mouth. It was something fresh and new and delicious. "What'd you think?" she asked. "Not what you expected, is it?"

A warmth flowed through my face. I was smiling, and even my smile felt different—sincere and real. "Yeah. That's not bad."

The music from the band stopped with a long screech from the harmonica and a few final licks from the guitar. Everyone on the dance floor clapped and hollered. A few people stomped their feet, begging the band not to quit.

"Time for their break, I better get back behind the bar." She stood up, reenergized. Her hands went again to my knees. "Promise me you'll stick around and talk to me later," she asked, but she already knew I would stay. This time, when she leaned in, she kissed me.

We lay in the hayfield, warm from the heavy summer air, the Mill's secret punch and the heat of our bodies. I discovered kissing Amanda was like flying. The dark skin on her arms and neck glowed silvery in the moonlight. Her body seemed even more unblemished and perfect.

The others had dragged limbs from the woods and built a little fire. Their shadows danced around the flame, but we had moved far enough away it seemed like we were alone. The guys from the band had brought their instruments, and if it was possible, they sounded even better out in the open field. At the bar, the band had performed their own songs, but here they pulled out their old favorites. Someone sang Bob Dylan's *Don't Think Twice, It's All Right*, with everyone joining in on the refrain. Their sounds settled over the field like the dew.

After a while, the music stopped, and then too their talking. Amanda and I settled into the stillness, no longer kissing. So much of the past few hours had gone between us without words. Our eyes had spoken for us at first, and later our ever-seeking hands. The silence between us had been comfortable and natural, and I didn't want to break it. We held each other and listened to the natural lullaby of the Saltville countryside playing around us – crickets and frogs trying to out-call each other, an owl at the edge of the woods, and the gentle roar of an occasional vehicle crossing nearby, hidden ridges. We were surrounded by a new kind of music that was wilder and more beautiful in its own way.

My fingers played across her flesh, but I still couldn't banish Michelle from my mind. Not completely at least. My fingers traced the length of Amanda's arm, and I couldn't help but to compare these two women, impossibly measuring one against the other until I realized tears were crawling down my cheeks.

I cried because I remembered the first time I had made love to Michelle and how it seemed to always get better for me every time afterward because it was familiar and common. I cried because I felt something with Amanda I never thought I'd feel again. And I cried because I felt ashamed. I was ashamed for crying like a child and more than anything for crying in front of Amanda. Before I could stop, her small voice, hardly more than a whisper, drowned out the night noises around us.

"She hurt you so bad," she said. "I'm so sorry."

It was the reaction I should have expected from her. She would never laugh or think less of me.

"You should tell me what Noah says. 'Everybody has problems. Deal with it.'" I pulled away from her, wiping the tears away with the back of my hand. "I'm sorry. I didn't mean to do this."

"What? Cry? Nothing wrong with showing a little bit of your soul every now and then."

I didn't know what to say. So I said nothing. She moved closer. Her arms tightened around me, unwilling to let me loose.

"I know you're thinking about her," she said. "It's all right."

"I *am* thinking about her, but I'm thinking about you too." And I was. "Mostly I was wondering if I could ever survive another broken heart."

"And now you wonder if you can trust me. Right? You're afraid I'll hurt you too." Her hand brushed my forehead and ran through my hair.

"When Michelle left, she said I didn't know who she was. When she said it, I thought she was crazy, but later, I began to think she was right. But now I think, maybe we can't really ever know someone else."

I lay completely flat on the ground and stretched my arms up to the heavens. I closed my eyes and blocked out the stars above me. She kissed me again, her warm mouth calling me to movement.

"What if I let you down?" I asked, unable to leave it alone.

"What if I let *you* down?" she asked back, smiling. We both knew that was really what I wanted to know.

Her eyes caught some light from above. I pulled the blanket around us, and we fell asleep in this field outside Saltville, under the biggest sky I had ever seen.

Redemption at Station Creek
by Sylvia Lynch

"Come on and go with me while I drown this cat." Powder Ausmus stood with his long fingers wrapped around the midsection of a skinny, wild–eyed tabby. The cat's body hung across his palm like a limp dishrag. Powder's other hand rested on his protruding hip bone. He was posed like one of those chalk dummies down in the window of Bailey's Dry Goods Store.

"Why do you want to drown that cat?" I asked.

"Cause old Miss Riley say this cat keep on leaving big turds in her begonias and she sick of it. She say he's becoming a nuisance and he got to go. She say she give me a quarter if I catch him and take him down there and drown him in Station Creek. I sure could use that quarter. So I caught him and now I'm fixing to go and drown him in the creek."

Powder could generally be counted on as a good source of diversion in an otherwise uneventful summer. I can't say we were friends. I spent a lot of time with him when school was not in session, but I never counted him among my buddies. Not like Sammy Grisby or the Fugate brothers were anyway. I think that's the way everybody around town felt about him. He was no more to most folks than that old maple tree in front of the courthouse or the rickety bridge across Clinch River. Nobody ever used that old bridge any more but it never occurred to anyone to get rid of it.

We didn't really know much about Powder or where he came from. He just showed up one July afternoon, almost like he had fallen out of the sky. A bunch of us boys were sitting in the alley behind Martin's Hardware waiting on the heat to die down. It was too hot to go fishing and there was not much else to do in the afternoons when you had no money. We were passing time discussing the finer points of dough balls verses red worms when pond fishing for sun grannies. We fell silent when we noticed a shimmering profile easing up the alley. As he drew closer, we stood up and for a time none of us said anything. His faded clothes hung on his bony frame like curtains. He didn't introduce himself or make any effort to explain his business. He just stood quietly looking at us until we picked up our conversation again. He listened for awhile, and then joined in like he'd been there all along.

We found out later that Powder had moved in with his Aunt Mae in an unpainted clapboard house over across the railroad tracks. He had an easy way about him and a natural way of blending into any gathering of people, invited or not. I never thought to ask him why he had moved here or how long he was planning on staying. One of the Fugate boys said he heard his folks got rid of him because they didn't want him any more. I thought Arliss Fugate was lying until I heard Mama tell my Aunt Connie that his folks had "turned him out" because they wanted rid of him.

I was shocked to hear that you could just decide to throw a person away like junk you no longer had any use for. The thought of such a thing hit me a lot harder than I was prepared for. That night I lay in bed thinking of all the implications of such a predicament. What if my folks caught onto the idea and just suddenly decided to turn me out? I knew I wouldn't fare as well as Powder seemed to be doing. And I was certain I wouldn't take it as well as he had. I had no relatives that I knew of that I would even think about going off to live with. Besides, I doubted any of them would take me in, especially if my own folks decided I was not worth keeping.

I wondered if Powder had done something to turn his parents against him. He seemed harmless enough. As my Uncle Jack often said of the old boy that helped him put up his tobacco every fall, "Well, he ain't the sharpest knife in the drawer, but he appears to be a well-intentioned feller."

I don't think Powder was stupid or mean or anything. He just appeared to me to be the kind of fellow who had to take a little more time than most to figure things out for himself. Surely his folks wouldn't turn him out just because he was a little slow.

Powder was a little odd looking, but he wasn't dog ugly or deformed or anything. Not bad enough to notice anyway. Except for being the skinniest human I ever saw, the only thing really outstanding about him was those clear blue eyes of his. Sometimes when he stared real hard at my face, I'd get a case of the willies. I asked Mama one time how come Powder had them funny looking blue eyes. I told her I'd never seen a colored boy with blue eyes, at least not around these parts. Mama told me to shut my mouth and so I did.

"You coming or not?" Powder asked, the cat dangling in his hand.

I decided going along with him was probably the best use of my time on such a stifling August afternoon.

"Yeah, I reckon I will. But, now, I ain't going to help you. I'm just intending to watch, and that's all," I said.

As we crossed the railroad tracks and eased down the slope to the creek, I glanced at the cat. His wilted legs swung in perfect rhythm with Powder's long steps. I thought that old cat was taking this whole thing pretty well in stride, considering everything. The way he was hanging on Powder's hand like that was kind of creepy. All at once I started thinking I wished I hadn't said I'd come along. I knew I was going to have to see it through, so I gathered my resolve and moved up to walk beside Powder.

When we got to the creek, Powder didn't even slow down until he was knee deep in the muddy water. He held that old tabby up to his face and stared right into the cat's eyes. That cat stared straight back at him. Their noses were almost touching. The cat didn't move a muscle, just looked at Powder. After what seemed like forever, Powder turned his head and looked at me. My mouth had gone suddenly dry and I felt uncomfortable looking at him. I began to kick at an old tire lying halfway out of the water. Two dragonflies darted on the green scum that lined the creek bank. I thought Powder would never move and I was suffering something fierce in the lingering silence.

"How do you reckon a feller should go about drowning a cat anyways?" he finally asked.

"Hell if I know," I said. "You're the one getting the quarter. Figure it out your own self."

Powder raised the cat high above his head. His shirt sleeve slid up his arm and scotched against his elbow. I expected he was going to try to sling it against a rock. I saw my daddy kill a nest of baby skunks one time by bashing their heads against a rock. I wasn't sure I wanted to watch Powder do that. Or maybe he was just getting wound up to push him down deep in the water. I was waiting for the cat to start kicking and clawing. But he just hung there. Waiting. I felt a little sick from the heat.

Powder eased the cat back down in front of his face. They stared at each other again for a while. Suddenly Powder turned around and slung the cat onto the bank on the opposite side of the creek. The cat landed square on his feet with a thud, twitched for a minute, then strolled off toward the railroad tracks. He never looked back. Powder watched him until he topped the hill and was out of sight. Then he turned and looked me straight in the face.

"I hear tell cat turds is supposed to be good for begonias anyways."

Murder at the Bridge Table
(a Lydia Stram Mystery)
by M. L. McCann

Police officer Lydia Stram eased through the crowd of women bridge players clustered inside the door of the card room at the Acadia Falls Country Club. Some stared at her, their faces grim, others wept, and a few looked frightened. Scanning each face, Lydia recalled her dad's advice. "At a crime scene, remember everyone, and always focus on the details." Her dad, Big Jim Stram, would have been proud knowing she'd joined the force, if only he'd lived.

"'Bout time you showed up," Sergeant Gerard Boudreaux said.

Lydia ignored him. Over the backs of two kneeling paramedics, she saw the bloated, blotchy face of her tennis partner, Ann Fontierri, whose life they were trying to save.

"Oh geez," Lydia muttered, sickened by the sight.

"Get it together," Boudreaux muttered. "You may be a rookie, but ya gotta act like a pro."

She glared at the fat sergeant, knowing he hadn't a clue when it came to professionalism. As the medics worked, Lydia focused on the scene. A pizza slice rested near Ann's thigh. Additional slices, a red pepper jar, and an overturned plate lay beneath the nearby table, its soiled cloth hanging askew.

She scanned the faces, spotting Barb Carlson, the restaurant's manager, standing by the door to the pro shop, watching. Unlike the shock and horror on the card players' faces, Barb looked smug. Among the bridge players, Lydia's friend, Jessie, stood nearby. Tears and mascara streaked her face. Lydia walked over and hugged her. "What happened?"

Jessie shuddered. "She took one bite of pizza and grabbed her throat. I asked if she was okay, but Ann couldn't answer me. She broke out in red welts, craned her neck, and lurched backwards onto the floor." Jessie sniffled. "Someone should notify Frank."

"I'll call him," Lydia responded. "Ann told me he was leaving town today for a short business trip."

Lydia spotted Ann's handbag on one of the tables. Inside it, she found Ann's cell phone and scanned it for Frank's number. She used her own phone to call him, but he didn't answer. At the beep she said, "Frank, Ann's had an accident. Please call me."

Just then, one of the paramedics looked up at Boudreaux and said softly, "She's gone."

Gone? How could her healthy, energetic friend die at age thirty-three? Lydia couldn't stop her tears. She stepped over to the paramedic, and asked, "Why does she look like this? What did she die of?"

"Looks like an allergic reaction to me," he said. "Her bracelet indicates an allergy to peanuts and olives."

Lydia looked at the pizza on the floor. There were no olives or peanuts on the pizza, or anywhere else in the room, for that matter. Nevertheless, she gathered the pizza into a take home box for evidence.

Boudreaux told the women, "I'll interview each of you in the dining room. Don't anybody leave beforehand." He turned to Lydia. "Why don't you make yourself useful? Maybe you can talk with the wait-staff, once you're done crying that is."

Lydia met with Barb in her small office. "You don't seem very upset by Ann's death."

Barb raised an eyebrow. "I hardly knew her. Why should I be upset?"

"If a club member died in the restaurant I managed, I'd be upset. Don't you think it will taint the restaurant's reputation—and yours?"

"I'll tell you what taints our reputation," Barb answered tartly, "having a member write a nasty letter about one of our waitresses. Your friend, Fontierri, did just that, and I lost a good waitress."

"Really? Who was that?"

"Melinda Frist. Why?"

Lydia jotted down the name on her pad. "May I have her address and phone number? I'll need to talk to her."

Barb retrieved the information from her files and gave it to Lydia. "I don't see why. Melinda had nothing to do with this. She was fired last week."

"Was there another reason you didn't like Ann?" Lydia asked.

Barb looked alarmed. "What do you mean?"

"It's just a gut feeling. You seem strangely indifferent to her death; an unusual reaction under the circumstances. Is there more to it than Ann's letter of complaint?"

Barb shrugged. "Fontierri was a troublemaker. That's all I care to say."

As Lydia drove to Melinda's apartment, she tried to remember everything Ann had said during their last tennis game. The important news was that she'd filed for divorce. She'd talked about it for months. Lydia remembered feeling glad. She never liked Frank. He always seemed like such a leech.

Between sets, Ann mentioned having a crush on a younger man. She hadn't shared many details, but did mention possibly going to London with him.

At Melinda's apartment, a young Hispanic woman answered the door. Her eyes locked on Lydia's uniform and she stepped back. A woman, wrapped in a blanket, walked toward the door. "Who is it, Dolores?" Her blonde hair was tousled and her red nose looked tender and sore. "Oh, hello Officer. What's going on?"

"Ms. Melinda Frist?" Lydia asked.

"Yes." The woman coughed.

"I'm Officer Stram. May I come in?"

"Tell her come back later," Dolores snapped. "You too sick."

Melinda raised a placating hand. "It's okay, Dolores. Come in, Officer."

Melinda sat on the sofa, curling her legs beneath her, and Dolores sat at the far end. Lydia chose the loveseat opposite them, placing her police cap on the coffee table cluttered with magazines, a pad of paper scribbled with notes, and cold medications.

Lydia pulled out her pencil and pad. "How well did you know Ann Fontierri?"

Melinda sniffled. "The bridge player? Why, has something happened?"

"Ann Fontierri died today at the country club."

Dolores's eyes widened and her hand flew to her mouth.

"I hardly knew her at all," Melinda said, her voice cold. "Why are you questioning me? The club fired me last week."

"We're speaking to everybody from the club who knew her," Lydia responded.

Melinda looked annoyed while Dolores appeared frightened.

Lydia asked, "Was Ann a difficult customer?"

"You mean other than complaining to my boss and getting me fired?" She laughed sarcastically. "Actually, she was easy to wait on–always ordered the same thing: sweet tea and the house pizza."

"Do you know why she complained about you?"

Melinda glanced at Dolores then faced Lydia, faking a smile. "Oh, I have my ideas, but I'd rather not say. Now that she's dead, I guess we'll never know."

"You need to be straight with me, Ms. Frist. This is a police investigation."

Melinda coughed. "Look, I'm really not feeling well." She sighed. "Since I wasn't even there, could we cut this short?"

"You're making a mistake by not telling me all that you know regarding Ann Fontierri's death."

Melinda scowled. "I have nothing more to tell."

Lydia stood. "We'll talk again." Lydia picked up her cap, and noticed a name written on Melinda's paper pad. The name had a familiar ring, but she couldn't place it.

"Who's Jack Sapphire?"

Melinda crumpled the notepaper. "Nobody important."

As Lydia drove home, thinking of the report she had to write, her cell phone rang.

"Lydia? It's Frank. What's happened?"

She inhaled deeply. "You sitting down, Frank? I've bad news. There was an accident at the club today. Ann's dead."

She expected to hear him gasp, or cry, or something. Instead his voice sounded calm. "That's terrible. I'll come home right away."

The words sounded right, but the emotion was wrong. "In that case, I'll come over tonight, say about eight?"

"Okay. If you want to."

Frank Fontierri answered the door wearing sweats and holding a bottle of Lazy Magnolia beer. He invited her in and they settled in the breakfast nook.

"You want a beer?" he asked.

"No thanks." Lydia laid her notepad on the table. "Frank, I'm terribly sorry about Ann." He nodded.

"You don't seem all that upset," Lydia observed. He took a swig of beer. "Knock it off, Lydia. You know perfectly well Ann and I weren't getting along. Hadn't for a long time. She filed for divorce last week. I was served this morning."

"I see." Lydia watched him. He seemed too cool, too comfortable with his wife's death. "So, what now, Frank?"

"Life goes on. I keep the house and my lifestyle, unlike the intended outcome of the divorce."

"Really? What would've been the results of your divorce?"

Frank stared over her head. "I'd have been broke. The house and even the cars are in her name. Everything's always been her way–her money, her friends, her parties. I guess, now it'll be my way."

"So, you'd have been broke. That gives you motive, Frank. I hope you have witnesses for your whereabouts at the time of her death."

Frank blanched. "Why would I need witnesses?"

Lydia's internal alarms went off. "Where were you, Frank?"

He drew a ragged breath, set his chin at a slightly defensive angle, and said quietly, "I was at the club. I saw her collapse."

"What?" Lydia practically screamed in surprise.

He gestured with both hands. "I know, I know. I should've come forward at the time. I couldn't. I needed time to think."

Lydia glared, "About what?"

He shook his head sadly. "I'd been told she was cheating on me with some guy from the club. I followed her there to see if she was really playing bridge. I watched from the pro shop." His voice cracked. "I saw her turn blue and collapse. I wanted to go to her, but I couldn't explain my presence. Besides, what difference would it have made?"

"What difference? She was dying!"

"Well, there was nothing I could do about that. But it wasn't my fault! You believe me, don't you, Lydia?"

Lydia shook her head. "I think you're a lying son of a bitch and I don't believe a word you say." She stood and strode to the door. Holding it half open, she looked back. "Get a good lawyer, Frank."

The next morning, Lydia walked into the club's lounge at half past eleven. The place was empty except for Ryan, the bartender, who stood at a wide credenza filling miniature tin pails with peanuts from a bin below its marble top. He smiled at her.

Lydia slid onto a stool, and a moment later, Ryan walked behind the bar. "What can I get you, Officer?"

Lydia smiled. "Can I order lunch in here?"

"Sure, need a menu?"

"No. I'll have the small house pizza and some coffee."

"Comin' up."

As Ryan poured coffee, Barb Carlson breezed in carrying an empty peanut pail. When she spotted Lydia, she frowned and ignored her, saying to Ryan, "This was left on the patio. What'll I do with it?"

"Put it on the credenza. Dolores will take care of it." He set Lydia's coffee in front of her. "Barb, did Jason hear from that London outfit?" Lydia looked up with interest.

Barb grinned. "Yep. End of the month, we leave for England," she said, sailing out of the room.

"London?" Lydia remarked. "Ann Fontierri mentioned someone going to London the other day."

Ryan winked at her. "Probably Barb's husband. Ann had a thing for him. Everybody, here at the club, knew it."

"No kidding? Wasn't Barb jealous?"

"Barb?" Ryan laughed. "Not likely. She and Jason are pretty tight. I had a feeling it was all in Ann's mind, not Jason's." He picked up a picture from behind the cash register and handed it to Lydia. "Look, here's a photo of everyone who works in food and beverage at the club. It was taken at the Christmas party. Those two look totally happy together, don't you think?"

Lydia studied the picture. There was an intimacy to the way Barb and Jason stood holding each other's hands. Unexpectedly, she recognized a face other than Melinda's. "Is this the same Dolores you just mentioned? I met her at Melinda's yesterday. She works here?"

Ryan nodded. "She's been here about eight months. Her English has improved, but not enough to wait tables. She busses, cleans the kitchen, fills the peanut bowls, that sort of thing."

Lydia studied the picture as she shook pepper flakes over her pizza and bit into the crust topped with fragrant cheese. Something about the photo bothered her. "It looks like it was all couples, except for Melinda and Dolores."

"Dolores doesn't know anybody in Acadia Falls, and Melinda, of course, wouldn't bring her boyfriend."

"Why not?"

Ryan looked uncomfortable. He shrugged. "I suppose you'd find out anyway. Maybe you already know that Melinda's been having an affair with Frank Fontierri for about a year. They've tried to keep it secret, but here at the club, gossip spreads pretty fast. Personally, I don't get what she sees in that creep."

Lydia's stomach lurched. "Frank and Melinda? Oh my God."

Still thinking about Frank's cheating on Ann, Lydia raised the glass shaker and stared at the contents. "Did Ann use pepper flakes on her pizza?"

Ryan nodded. "Always. She liked it spicy."

Lydia nodded. "I need to take all the shakers for testing."

"All of them? Can't you leave us one at least?"

"Afraid not."

Ryan frowned. "Okay, I'll get them."

After lunch, Lydia walked into Chief Ray's office and found Boudreaux there.

Chief Ray gave her a nod. "Boudreaux and I were just discussing the Fontierri case. He thinks she died from choking on her pizza."

Lydia shook her head as she placed the pepper jars on Chief Ray's desk. "No way. She was murdered."

Boudreaux sighed. "Oh great, here comes another, crazy Lydia Stram theory."

Chief Ray raised an eyebrow. "Talk to me, Lydia."

"Like my dad said, it's always in the details, Chief. Ann ordered the club's pizza every time she played cards there and always sprinkled it with pepper flakes. She frequently warned the wait–staff that she was allergic to peanuts. I think someone killed her by mixing crushed peanuts into those pepper jars."

"I don't know where you come up with this cockamamie crap," Boudreaux muttered.

"Who do you suspect?" Chief Ray asked.

"Well, Barb Carlson may have been jealous of Ann because she was making a play for Barb's husband," Lydia said. "But I'm looking more at Melinda Frist and Frank Fontierri. I just haven't figured out how either of them could have gotten the peanuts into the shakers."

"Ignore her Chief. She ain't got a shred of evidence to back it up," Boudreaux groused.

"Should be easy enough to prove, one way or the other," Lydia said. "Let's test these shakers for peanut shavings, along with the pizza I brought from the crime scene. In the meantime, let's bring in all the suspects for you to question, Chief."

Chief Ray nodded. "Good idea. Go round 'em up tout–la–suite. That means right now in Cajun, Boudreaux."

"I know what it means, Chief. Okay, Stram," he smirked. "Let's go get your suspects so I can watch your theory sink like a holy boat in the bayou."

An hour later, Lydia studied the suspects sitting outside Chief Ray's office waiting to be interviewed. Melinda held a box of tissues due to her lingering cold. Barb seemed impatient as she flipped through a magazine. Frank buried his face in a book, refusing to look at anyone. Apparently, he'd taken Lydia's advice and brought his lawyer, who sat reading *USA Today*. The only one who appeared worried was Dolores, and she seemed downright frightened.

As Lydia watched Dolores gnaw at her fingernails, she recalled where she'd heard Jack Sapphire's name. She crossed the room and sat down beside Dolores. "I know you're in this country illegally." Dolores didn't respond. "I saw Jack Sapphire's name scribbled on notepaper on Melinda's coffee table. He's a forger specializing in immigration papers. My dad arrested him in Tupelo ten years ago. I'm surprised he's out of jail.

"Melinda discovered you're an illegal, too, didn't she?" Dolores glanced at Melinda who glared back at her. "Melinda forced you to poison Mrs. Fontierri, didn't she? She threatened to turn you over to immigration unless you mixed crushed peanuts into the red pepper shakers."

Dolores jumped to her feet, her hands fisted. "I no want to! Melinda say peanuts no kill, only scare her—make her sick."

Melinda leapt up, pointing her finger at Dolores. "Shut up, you lying little tramp. I tried to help you, and this is how you repay me?"

Before long, Frank and Barb and everyone else were shouting accusations and threats at each other. It took both Lydia and Boudreaux to subdue them.

An hour later, after Melinda and Dolores were booked into the jail, Chief Ray asked Lydia how she'd figured it out.

"It all made sense after I found out about Melinda and Frank's affair, but it really fell into place when I remembered who Jack Sapphire was. I eliminated Barb when she said she and her husband were leaving for London. From what I observed, she wasn't threatened by Ann's crush on Jason.

"Melinda wanted Ann out of the way so she and Frank could be together. Frank wasn't served divorce papers until the morning he left town—I checked—the same morning Ann died. So Melinda had no knowledge of the divorce when she plotted Ann's death. Even though Melinda no longer had access to the pepper jars, Dolores did. Knowing Dolores was an illegal, I figured Melinda blackmailed her into putting the crushed peanuts into the pepper shakers.

"I wasn't sure about Frank's innocence until Dolores pointed the finger at Melinda this morning, and the shouting began. Although it doesn't change the fact he's a total ass."

Boudreaux nodded. "I knew it all along. I could tell that little Mexican was the murderer. She had that suspicious look."

Chief Ray rolled his eyes. "Good detective work, Officer Stram."

"Thanks Chief. But, I had a little help from my dad."

Bluebirds or Buzzards
by Annie B. McKee

It all started last Friday morning when Momma Mertis was leaving *Gloria's Little Touch of Magic* beauty salon. It was one of those beautiful bluebird sky mornings and Momma Mertis was pretty well tuckered out. 'Cause you see, it takes a little more than magic sometimes to glam-up Momma Mertis. She walked through the graveled parking lot, *crunch, crunch, crunch,* as she headed for her Ford Escort, and all of a sudden Jimmie Jane slid her car right into the parking space right next to Momma's piece of junk. Momma's jaw dropped as she saw her next-door-neighbor for the last fifty-seven years driving a brand new Mercury Sable. It was a bright Tornado red, which happened to be Momma's favorite color. Now Momma Mertis had been looking and drooling at this very car for weeks down at the Mercury place. It just didn't set right with Momma Mertis that Jimmie Jane was now the proud owner of the most beautiful car in the whole world.

As Momma Mertis was getting into her car, Jimmie Jane beamed proudly and shouted, "Hey Mertis Claudia! Did you see my new car?"

"Oh, is that a new car?" Momma Mertis asked innocently enough.

"Why yes, just picked it up this morning."

"Ah, well, it's nice," Momma Mertis, mumbled while trying to make her getaway before Jimmie Jane got into one of those long drawn out yackety–yaks, because, boy, could she talk. Not that Momma Mertis was short changed in the conversing department.

Before Momma Mertis could get her car door slammed, Jimmie Jane was out of her new and dazzling automobile and stood face–to–face with Momma. She never missed a breath as she continued to talk lickity split.

"Oh, Mertis Claudia, I have so much to do this morning. Besides picking up my new car, (she had to mention that again) and after I get my hair done, I've got to meet little Junie Jane (that's Jimmie Jane's miserable little great grand) to take her to the high school. You know today at four o'clock is the final signup for the *Miss Magnolia Blossom* contest. It's too bad Mertis Mandy couldn't be there to see Junie Jane crowned."

We–l–l, you could have knocked Momma over with a feather! Suddenly Momma Mertis was hotter than a pan of scalded water. Momma slammed her car door shut and took off in a cloud of smoke. No, Momma Mertis didn't screech off too fast out of the dusty graveled parking lot, but the smoke was because she was way past due on having the oil changed. She thought, *I've just got to get this car to the shop, but not today. I've got too much to do.*

She left Jimmie Jane standing in the parking lot with a question mark plastered upon her face as Momma Mertis drove down Friendship Lane past the First Baptist Church where she and Jimmie Jane were longtime members of the *Love Thy Neighbor* Sunday School class and around the corner to her driveway.

"Harrumph, where does Jimmie Jane get the idea that Junie Jane is *Miss Magnolia Blossom* material? Why that kid looks too much like Jimmie Jane to have a chance."

Momma threw the car into park and ran into the house. She picked up the telephone in one mighty movement, and dialed the number. She prepared to bring forth her soft and silky voice and in a charming manner.

"Hello there," Momma Mertis said in a sparkling mood.

"Hi," answered Mertis Mandy's Mom.

"Oh, I'm so glad to have caught you at home. I have some marvelous news."

"What is it?"

"You know the exciting *Miss Magnolia Blossom* contest for high school girls?"

"Ah, yes, I do." Mertis Mandy's Mom waited for the next sentence out of Momma's mouth.

"Oh, terrific, because today is the last day to register for participation, and I thought little Mertis Mandy might be interested in winning, with me, of course, as her advisor and sponsor."

"Well, Momma Mertis, we can ask Mandy, err, I mean, Mertis Mandy (in the presence of Momma Mertis, one must always call the great granddaughter her full name of Mertis Mandy–her namesake, you know).

"Okay, when will she be home from school?"

"Anytime now. I'll have her call you."

"Well," Momma Mertis continued without a breath, "Mertis Mandy will be a favorite with the crowd, I just know. Why with her dazzling good looks and talent–all passed down through the family genes, not to mention her intellect and outgoing personality." Momma Mertis paused for a quick breath when she heard over the telephone that the door slammed and a lively little voice could be heard. "Oh, is that little Mertis Mandy now?"

"Why, yes it is. I'll hand the phone to her."

"Hello, Mertis Mandy. I hope you had a good day at school."

"Yes, Momma Mertis. It was super."

"Oh good Dear. Hmm, I wanted to let you know that this afternoon is time to signup for the *Miss Magnolia Blossom* pageant."

"It is?" Mandy asked innocently.

"Yes, and I hoped you would be interested in participating."

"Well, sure Momma Mertis, if you think I can qualify."

"Qualify? Why Baby Girl you will be the leader of the whole bunch."

Mertis Mandy giggled.

Momma Mertis pushed a little harder. "You go and get all prettied up and I will pick you up in about fifteen minutes, okay?"

"Well, okay Momma Mertis, if you're sure?"

Twenty minutes later Momma Mertis and Mertis Mandy arrived at the high school. The ride en route was actually a primer course for the contest strategies that were all drilled out by Momma Mertis. This wasn't the Miss Mississippi contest, but pretty close, so everything had to be planned just perfect.

Upon arrival at the school, Momma Mertis parked right close to a shiny red Mercury Sable, which she might have put a big dent into by opening her door real hard. Inside the school, the very first people that Momma Mertis spied were Jimmie Jane and Junie Jane as they stood at the signup desk.

"Oh, hi," squealed Junie Jane.

"Hi," Mertis Mandy grabbed her friend. "Isn't this exciting?"

Before Mertis Mandy could say anything else, Momma Mertis whispered into her ear, "Don't get too chummy Baby Girl. Remember, Junie Jane is a competitor now."

"Oh-ooo," Mertis Mandy said quietly.

About that time, Jimmie Jane whirled around and with narrowed eyes hissed, "There will be no more chit–chat until this contest is final and Junie Jane is declared her rightful place as *Miss Magnolia Blossom.*"

"Oh, yeah," squawked Momma. "We'll see who the winner is, after all its winner material that is necessary as it is cultivated through the family genes."

With that both great grandmothers grabbed their respective girls by the hand and marched out. The girls were wide–eyed and confused, but the great grandmothers knew exactly what they were doing and it will be blood to the very end!

The morning of the *Miss Magnolia Blossom* contest appeared warm, sunshiny, and beautiful. The weatherman had not forecasted any storms, but at the high school the winds–of–war were brewing full steam.

Momma Mertis and Mertis Mandy arrived at the school auditorium bright and early.

"Momma Mertis, are you sure about this dress for the formal wear competition?" Mertis Mandy asked.

"Oh, you can never go wrong with sequins and feathers," advised Momma Mertis.

"But, but, but," Mertis Mandy tried.

"There will be no buts, Baby Girl. You will be the winner, no doubt."

Yes, things did go exceedingly well for Mertis Mandy and Junie Jane. At the end, the contest was down to three finalists with Mertis Mandy and Junie Jane placed among the three. The third contestant, Melanie Walters, didn't have a skunk's chance thought both Momma Mertis and Momma Jimmie. This unfortunate girl's great grandmother lived out of state, so the poor dear did not have the benefit of the great grandmotherly guidance.

Everyone was seated on the edge of their chairs as the Master of Ceremony, School Principal Mr. Wilson, cleared his throat for the grand announcement.

"Ladies and gentlemen, we will take the liberty of adverting from the normal protocol by announcing the winner first and the runners up last. Let me assure you that the decision of the winner was easy. It's the choice of the runners up that was confusing and unsettling. So without further delay, the winner of the *Miss Magnolia Blossom* contest is Melanie Walters and tied for third place is Miss Mertis Mandy McLemore and Miss Junie Jane Culpepper."

"What do you mean tied for third place?" shouted both Momma Mertis and Momma Jimmie. "What happened to second place?"

"Err, uh, well," stammered Mr. Wilson. "This was a unique situation. I mean this year for the *Miss Magnolia Blossom* contest it just seemed more prudent to make this decision for all concerned." Then Mr. Wilson practically ran out a side door and "whish" disappeared.

Mertis Mandy and Junie Jane squealed and jumped for joy that they had been named third place runners up and then ran to Melanie as they gushed their congratulations and hugs to their friend.

Momma Mertis and Momma Jimmie eyed each other with an air of continued competition.

Momma Mertis shouted, "I demand a recount."

Jimmie Jane snorted, "This contest should be declared in contempt."

You see, both Momma Mertis and Momma Jimmie watch Judge Judy and Court TV everyday. They know fraud and trickery when they see it!

Now you know why that on this beautiful bluebird morning Momma Mertis is in one of her buzzard moods. But after all tomorrow is another day, and the TV Community Calendar just announced that the registration for the *Miss Moonlight Serenade* contest has begun. Momma Mertis can be heard humming a little tune as she dialed the telephone.

"Hello, little Mertis Mandy. I've just heard some marvelous news."

The Package
by Terry Miles

The small gift-wrapped package lay on the wrought iron table in the Winslow kitchen unopened. Each time twenty–five year old Julie Hanson passed by she paused to finger the twine that held the bright tissue. Sometimes she would lift it, but never would she dare to open it.

"Julie, are you almost ready to go?" yelled Mollie, Julie's younger sister, as she pushed the front door open.

"I'm in the kitchen."

"You really need to lock the front door."

"I know, I know. That was one of dad's strictest rules. With all that's going on I just forgot." She turned to her sister and they hugged tightly.

When they stepped back Mollie observed, "You still haven't opened it."

"What?"

"You know," Mollie said, pointing toward the gaily wrapped present.

"Maybe ... maybe later."

"Sure. I understand." Mollie moved toward the kitchen windowsill which held the framed picture of three men in uniform. "Would you look at them? Our three men; Dad, our brother Kurt, and your husband Jason."

Julie moved to lean against her sister. "Aren't they something?"

"Yeah! The caption at the bottom says it all. 'Livin' it up in Baghdad. Wish you were here.'" Julie sighed deeply. "I can remember when we drove the three of them to the airport."

"I drove because you didn't feel well. Dad guessed it right off the bat. Of course Kurt didn't get it at first, but Jason was shocked!"

Julie smiled. "That's right. He asked 'Are you sure?'"

"Then Daddy yelled 'I'm going to be a grandpa!'"

"And Kurt screamed, 'My God, I'll be an uncle!'"

There was a knock on the screen door, followed by the doorbell. "I'll get it," Mollie said.

At the door she said, "Hello Sergeant Williams."

"Good morning Ms. Winslow. Is Mrs. Hanson ready?"

"I believe so. Come in and I'll get her. Julie?"

"I'll be there in a minute." Julie looked at the picture again, remembering her dad coming home with orders to Iraq. Two weeks later Kurt arrived from boot camp with the same orders. Then she thought about Jason. He had come tip-toeing through their house and surprised her in the bedroom. He told her he had planned a candlelit dinner for the two of them on the patio. After they had eaten he presented her with a tiny heart-shaped locket ... and his news. He was being deployed. Destination unknown. But they both knew. She remembered how he held her close. Very close.

Mollie joined her again in the kitchen. "Sergeant Williams is waiting."

"Mollie," Julie gestured with outstretched arms. "Do you remember when Jason painted this kitchen?"

"How could I forget? He stepped off the bottom rung of the ladder and right into the paint pan! It splattered all over the tile floor, walls, and Daddy!"

"Daddy was so angry."

"He was as mad as a wet cat."

"Jason apologized ten times over."

"Yeah. Daddy told him he wished for him to have his own son just as clumsy. Julie, we'd better leave."

"I know, I know."

Riding in the back seat of the sedan, Julie gazed out the window. The sky was robin egg blue. Jason's eyes were the same color blue. It was twenty-five miles into town and another three to the funeral at the chapel where she and Jason had married four years ago. She remembered when she was first introduced to Jason by her brother Kurt. At first she was appalled by his manners. But as time passed, he grew on her.

Her daddy liked him right off. Soon it was the five of them going fishing at Cainy Creek or swimming at Johnson's Bend. They did everything together. Bowling, movies and hiking. A year later he asked her dad for her hand in marriage. Dad said his only regret was that Mom hadn't lived to see the wedding.

"What are you thinking about?" Mollie asked.

"Do you remember when Dad and Mom brought Kurt home to live with us?"

Mollie laughed. "Of course! You said they should have just left him where they found him, that you didn't want a brother. But after his parents were killed he became our brother by adoption."

"Yeah, and he turned out to be the best brother ever."

When they arrived at the chapel Sergeant Williams held the door open for them. In the middle of the room the flag draped coffins were the only color in the white–washed chapel. Julie and Mollie clung to each other on the porch, staring in the door. Two officers came up to greet them.

"Mrs. Hanson, Miss Winslow, allow me to introduce Captain Hendrix and Lieutenant Lucas." The two officers saluted and bowed to the women.

"Your father, brother, and husband spoke often of you both," the Captain said. "Would you like us to escort you inside?"

Mollie glanced at her sister who shook her head. "If you don't mind, we'd like to enjoy the cool breeze a moment more."

"Of course. Just let us know when you're ready."

The soldiers left them alone on the porch, staring out at the yard. Mollie withdrew the small package and presented it to her sister. "Julie, I think you should open this now."

Julie's eyes flooded with tears. "You had no right to bring this. It's not yours."

"He sent it to you, Sis. It must be important."

Julie took the gift and clutched it to her chest, tears flowing down both their cheeks. Sergeant Williams came outside and touched her lightly on the shoulder.

"The Chaplain says we're ready."

Just as she was about to enter the chapel, Julie noticed the silhouette of a soldier hobbling towards her on crutches. Straining her eyes, her mouth dropped in recognition.

She ran to him, grabbing him and hugging tightly.

"Jason! Oh, Jason, it's you! It's really you!"

"They just released me from the hospital this morning. Did you receive the package?"

"Yes, of course. But it didn't say who had sent it, just that it came from Baghdad. Was it from you?"

"No, it's from your dad. Where is it?"

Both women were hugging and kissing him, as he leaned on them for support. All three of them were alternately laughing and crying. When they had calmed just a bit Jason asked again, "Where's the package?"

Julie brought it out and worked at the coarse twine that held together the brightly printed tissue paper. Inside she found a tiny black box that she opened nervously. There, nestled between two squares of cotton, was a silver charm that read "#1 Grandpa." As she clutched it between her fingers, she felt dizzy and leaned into Jason.

"It's time to begin the service," Sergeant Williams called from the porch.

They entered the chapel and Julie continued towards the front, stopping at her father's coffin. She leaned forward and kissed it, whispering, "I love you Daddy. Thank you for the gift." Taking the few steps to her brother's coffin, she leaned and kissed it as well. "Kurt, I'll tell our son every day about his brave Uncle."

Two months later Jason and Julie had their baby boy. They named him Kenneth Kurt Hanson.

Goose Chase
by Jan Rider Newman

The only thing Val ever wanted to do was farming. His family never owned any land, so they sharecropped for others. Since the age of nineteen, Val had worked for Norman Fontenot. Norman owned a lot of land north of Bayou Nezpique, and he let it out to four sharecroppers, including Val. Spring and summer were the busiest times, and during winter there was livestock to tend, houses to repair and paint, and equipment to get into shape for the spring. There was also spare time for his tenants and their wives to sit in drafty frame houses with space heaters turned up all the way and windows rattling in the late January wind. It blew all winter over flat, gray fields that not even sunshine cheered up. And when the men sat, they thought about Norman and his family in their pine-paneled den with the TV showing them the world.

So Norman always organized something when January got long and tiresome. One year he arranged a deer hunt, another year a catfish fry. The year after that, his daughter couldn't have picked a better month than January to get married, and we all went to the wedding. 1960 was the year of the goose hunt.

Norman pulled into our driveway just before dark one Tuesday in his new red Chevy truck. I lit the burner under the coffee pot and stepped out on the porch to invite him inside.

"No thanks, Emmy. Is Val home?" He stood in the yard and hitched his jeans over his skinny hips.

I started to ask him couldn't he see Val's pickup right beside him. "He's milking," I said.

Norman headed around the house, and I went back to patting out biscuits. High above the roof I heard geese honk. A flock had settled in a field close by, and at sunrise this morning they woke us up with their racket. Once the geese flew past, I kept listening. All I heard were the ticks the oven made as it heated up. Nothing else in the house made a sound. At this time of day, and especially this part of the year, I missed the noises of children. Val and I never had any. Now that we were in our late forties, I knew we never would. Val had his fields and his farming, and every other woman I knew had kids and grandkids to fuss over and brag about. I had Val and our house, which I painted inside every couple of years–yellow in the kitchen, blue in the bedrooms, white everywhere else–and kept the cabinets and furniture polished and the glass sparkling.

That day, just after I set the biscuits in the oven, I glanced out the back window and saw Norman and Val step out of the barn, heavy in talk. As more geese flew over, they pointed at them. Then Norman drove off, and Val carried in the milk pail.

"Norman says if we get us a good mess of geese this week he'll throw a supper Saturday night and buy all the beer and rice and stuff."

"Okay."

He took the strainer down from its hook on the wall and started pouring warm milk through it into the jugs I had scalded. We didn't talk for a few minutes. I turned the chicken frying on the stove, and Val got the milk into the refrigerator. He walked toward the bathroom, dropping the straps of his overalls and unbuttoning his shirt. "Damn, Emmy. You ain't got the heater on in here."

In the bathroom doorway I felt the contrast from the warmth in the kitchen. Not only did the air raise goose bumps, but my feet and ankles chilled from the wind blowing under the floor.

"I'm sorry. I was daydreaming." The paper from my brother's letter crackled in my apron pocket. "I heard from Ray today."

Val turned a handle at the sink and waited for the water to run warm. "They doing all right?"

"They're fine. Val, any time you're ready he can get you on at Conoco in Lake Charles."

"Emmy."

"We could have a brick house on a slab and a new Buick sedan every couple of years like my brother."

Val soaped his hands and wrists. "I'm not moving to Lake Charles, Emmy. I'm where I want to be." He yanked the towel off the nail next to the sink. "Why do you have to bring this up all the time? You know how I feel."

"What about how I feel? I want us to have something. Is that so wrong? Ray has a good retirement plan. On Social Security we'll never have better than what we got now, and you know it."

It was an argument I had never won, and that night was no different. Eventually, I did what I always did. I gave up and waited for another day.

Early next morning Val took down his shotgun and went after geese, but they flew away like they had heard talk of the supper. He came in with one, and the other men didn't do any better. Only one of them was worth a hang with a shotgun, and he was laid up with a broken ankle. Even so, he wanted to get up until his wife offered to give him another cracked bone. Fifteen people in all would be at the supper, and three geese wouldn't make the rounds. There was talk of Norman and Pam killing one of their turkeys or some hens.

Then, at sunset Friday, a big flock of snow geese glided into the fallow field half a mile behind the house. They made a cloud against the blue–red sky. You could tell they were nervous, though, circling and circling, starting up at the least noise. Val and I stood on the back porch and watched them.

"You'll have a time getting some in the morning," I said. I wanted to get supper over with so I could get to my cousin's bridal shower. I also had one other thing on my mind.

"Do you know what Bobby Comeaux told me when I was in Nezpique yesterday? He's selling his grocery store and wants three thousand down."

Val kept watching the geese. "Yeah, I heard that."

"You know, Val, he does a good business. He's going to live with his daughter because he's getting crippled with arthritis."

Val glanced at me. "Yeah."

"You've been with Norman thirty years, and we have good credit at the bank. We could get a loan for that down payment."

"I thought that's where this was going."

"Why not? Come on, Honey. This is our chance. If Bobby Comeaux can run a store on a ninth grade education–"

"And I got less than that."

"I have more. Val, the two of us can do it. Betty LeBleu works for Bobby a few days a week. She could help us get started. And the people around here know us. They'll buy from us. There's the house in the back. We'd have us a place of our own for the rest of our lives."

I squeezed his arm. "And the best part is you could keep on farming. You'd have to, so we could make payments."

Val pushed his hat back and thought a minute, his age and weather wrinkles smoothing out as if he was stretching the idea in his mind to see it all.

"You farm as long as you want," I said, "and I'll run the store myself."

He shook his head. "We're too old to learn how to run a business."

"We're not even fifty. Now, listen to me. You've had everything like you wanted it all these years. You want to farm, fine. I'm not asking you to quit this time. But my mind is made up about that store. I need something to keep me busy, too, and we don't have kids, so this is it."

This time Val quit arguing, which wasn't the same as agreeing, but it was something new. I drove to the shower in Nezpique after supper and left as soon as I could because my mind stayed on the store. On the outskirts of town, I pulled over and looked at the source of my hopes, a white wooden building in need of paint, but solid, with a new roof. There was an overhang between the store front and the two Phillips 66 gas pumps. Gravel and squashed soda pop cans covered the driveway under the overhang. I looked at the Coca-Cola thermometer and the cracked rubber gaskets hanging on each side of the double screen doors and the heaped up tires, inner tubes, crates, feed sacks, and such that had piled up over the years.

I saw Val and me cleaning up, painting, making the store ours. Owning it was right for us. I felt it like smooth cream in my mouth. Ours. Mine.

I shifted into first and took off for home, winding along the dark, narrow roads.

Val should have been waiting up, half asleep in his rocking chair. The lights were on, but he wasn't in the house. He didn't answer when I called for him outside.

While I was standing on the porch, a truck drove past. In the light from the yard lamp I saw wildlife patrol markings on the driver's door, and a thought hit me. I ran inside. A quick look on the bedroom wall where Val kept his shotgun told me what I needed to know.

The flashlight was missing, too, so I took off in the moonlight without changing out of my good black coat, best dress, new stockings, and Sunday pumps. I ran across the fields toward the place where we saw the geese settle. I stumbled and twisted my ankles in holes and tractor ruts and cut my legs and hands on dried grass stubble and barbed wire fences. All I could think of was getting to Val before he fired a shot.

Then I heard boom–boom, boom–boom. Two guns. What other fool was out there with Val? I screamed his name, but I might as well have saved my breath, what with the guns firing again and the racket from the geese that rose into the air all at once. As I got closer to the spot where the shooting came from, geese flew in a panic right over me. Then I saw flashlight beams, and a big, dark thing almost knocked me down. I caught it and hung on.

"Val?"

"I got no gun. Don't–I give up–what?"

"Norman?" I shook him by the front of his jacket. "Where's Val?"

"Emmy?" All I saw were the whites of his eyes. "I got to get out of here. Let go."

I hung on harder. "Tell me where Val is."

"He ran the other way. Come on, Emmy, let go. I'm sorry. I–I'm sorry." He tore free of my hands and ran away.

"Sorry for what? Was this your idea?" I yelled after him.

I tried to decide whether to look for Val some more or go home, and that's when I saw another dark shape and heard steps crunch on the stubble. Before I could call out, a game warden switched on his flashlight and shined it in my face.

"What are you doing out here?" He flipped his light up and down as if to get a good look at me. I guess he wanted to make sure I didn't have a gun, but I thought of my shredded stockings and muddy shoes and coat.

"A man ran this way," he said. "I heard you talking. Who was he? Where did he go?"

"A–a man? Uh, yeah, but I don't know who. It was too dark. I'm out here looking for my dog. She's a little bitty Chihuahua, and she's in heat, and–"

"You'd better go home, lady." After the warden took off after Norman, I ran the other way to hunt for Val.

Splashes in the flooded part of the field and the moonlight shining on white, floating blobs led me to him. I called real low.

"Norman?" he answered. "Come help me."

"Fool, he's halfway home by now. It's me."

"Emmy? What the hell?"

"Let's get out of here. A game warden saw me and went after Norman. Get out of that water. Throw down those birds."

"I told you, they're gone. It'll be okay as long as we don't show no more lights." He handed me his shotgun and waded back out with his canvas sack. "We must've got a dozen."

Shivering in the wind, I thought I ought to leave him there. "You are going to pay me for this, Val."

Then a heavy hand landed on my shoulder. I hadn't heard anyone else coming. Slowly, I turned to face a second game warden.

"You'd better let me have that shotgun," he said.

"I wasn't–this isn't–" I handed it over.

"Here's another one," Val called. "Hoo, Emmy, look how big."

He turned toward me, holding up the goose. It was so big and so white with its wings spread out, I thought of angels. The warden switched on his flashlight. I saw a trickle of red on the breast feathers, and Val saw us. For a long time he didn't move or say anything, only stood there in the water. Then he waded over and set down the bag and the great big goose.

Betty LeBleu bought the store, and I went to work for her. I made enough to pay our illegal hunting fines, Val's and mine. The game wardens never caught Norman. He gave me an old car for next to nothing, payment for keeping his name out of it, I guess, so I drove it back and forth to work. I quit talking about my brother and moving to Lake Charles, or doing anything but farming and working in a store and retiring on Social Security.

One of the first big things I bought with my paycheck was a TV. Val and I loved Dick Van Dyke, *Gunsmoke*, and *The Munsters*. We learned about the marches on Selma and Washington. We saw John F. Kennedy assassinated in Dallas, Martin Luther King killed in Memphis, and students gunned down by the National Guard in Ohio. Images of women burning their bras and men their draft cards mixed with footage on the war in Vietnam. We wondered what the world was coming to.

On July 20, 1969, Val slept as the Eagle landed and the first human beings made footprints on the moon. I started to wake Val, but he had said it was all a fake, so I let him sleep and watched by myself. I leaned forward in my chair, straining to hear every word from Neil Armstrong and Buzz Aldrin, to see their every stride, every hop, and to separate the astronauts from their ghost images. My eyes kept focusing on the flag they planted, the American flag sticking straight out to the side. No wind, no air to move it.

The program didn't last as long as I'd hoped, or show as much as I wanted to see. I turned off the set, restless and wanting something. I wandered into the kitchen and lifted the top off my cake saver, but I didn't want any cake. I didn't want a drink of water either. I opened the back door and stepped outside.

Over the years I had stood out here many times, watching the land in the dark, watching the stars in the sky. Now I watched the moon and wished I could see that far, wished I could be there with the astronauts. All I saw was the same old moon, the same old land. I heard the milk cow munching grass in the pen and smelled the sweet, grassy smell of her fresh droppings.

Val walked out through the screen door, yawning, and rested his arm around my shoulders. "Can you see them up there?"

"No."

"There's nobody up there," he said.

"I think there is."

We looked at each other in the dark then he slapped a hand to the side of his face just as I heard a whine near my left ear. The mosquitoes had found us.

"Come on, old woman," Val said. "Let's go to bed."

After we turned off the light and climbed under the sheet, Val said, "Do you still regret the store?"

"The store? We haven't brought that up in a long time."

"Do you?"

"I don't know. Sometimes. Betty says she'll probably have to close it next year. With all those supermarkets opening in the bigger towns, no one wants to pay what she has to ask for the groceries."

"She's been saying that for years."

"I think she means it now."

"What'll you do if she closes up?"

"Find another job, I guess."

Val sighed. "I'm sorry things didn't work out the way you wanted."

"Are you, Val? I think things work out for the best sometimes." I patted his shoulder. "It's okay, old man, go to sleep."

He rolled over and did just that. I lay on my back and thought about the moon. I thought about Michael Collins, who didn't get to go with Armstrong and Aldrin but had to wait in the orbiting capsule and make sure it was okay and help his friends come back to it safely. That was his job. Maybe he chose the job, or someone told him to take it or leave it. Maybe he complained but did it anyway.

I whispered, "God bless Michael Collins," just before I fell asleep.

Truth and Mercy
by Richelle Putnam

The first time Daddy struck my mama, he threatened to kill her. The second time, he did.

Burrowed up under our kitchen table, I watched Daddy fling a chair across the room. It splintered like broken bones. Mama hurled her beer bottle at him and it splattered against the wall. Beer streamed down like tears. Then, Daddy opened the cabinet above the refrigerator, the one where all the liquor was, and pulled out the revolver he kept hidden back there. Mama didn't flinch, like she dared him to pull the trigger. He grabbed her, pressed the barrel against her head. The room started closing in, squeezing me tight until I couldn't breathe, but I couldn't take my eyes from that silvery metal against Mama's head, her eyes beginning to plead, her mouth saying nothing.

I charged out, screaming, arms flailing like I was chasing a bunch of crows out of the soybean field. I heard the thump of Mama dropping to the floor. Daddy froze, his wild eyes bulging like someone was inside his head kicking them of their sockets.

He hadn't shot her, but struck her head with the butt of the gun. And she wasn't moving. Blood oozed through her silky hair, creating a bloody pillow. I knelt, dragged her limp body onto my lap, a bloody trail following her on the floor.

She was dead. I started rocking her, making up a song like she always did for me. "Hush, little mama, don't you cry. I'll get him back by and by."

The medics finally arrived to pry me from my mama, me kicking and hitting. Mama was dead. Daddy had killed her.

Family Services stuck me in a group home. Day after day, the tall, wiry prosecutor in a black suit forced me to relive that day, Mama dead in my arms, daddy sniveling, "I didn't mean to kill her."

Traitors were everywhere in the courtroom, Daddy's friends, even some of Mama's friends, all saying Mama's betrayal had compelled my daddy's rage.

I jumped up from my seat yelling, "That's a lie."

A black lady in a uniform dragged me out, and she wiped my tears, saying, "Everything's going to be all right."

Lies.

Daddy was sentenced to ten years for involuntary manslaughter. Ten years for my mama's life. I hated my daddy more that day than the day he murdered my mama.

None of Daddy or Mama's family or friends wanted me or my deep-seeded problems. This is when I learned what family meant—absolutely nothing.

I ripped up every letter I received from Parchman Penitentiary. I didn't want a paper daddy. I wanted my beautiful mama with her flowing black hair, mysterious eyes, and graceful butterfly arms. Mama had always been there for me and my chest ached like it had been blown to bits. Daddy had never been around anyway, always in the field, or away hunting or fishing or drinking with his buddies.

Daddy kept writing. I kept shredding. A year passed before Preacher Man first visited me. I remember how the sunlight through the window in the great room washed over him, creating the vision of an angel. He stood when he saw me, smiled as if he'd always known me. To this day, I don't why I didn't refuse him like I had refused the others trying to save me from my wretched self.

We strolled through gardens planted to soothe the restless and sat on an iron bench surrounded by lilies and gladiolas. Flowers always returned me to Mama's grave where I had cried out, "Don't leave me, Mama." That day, a stranger's arms held me back from the hole where Mama's casket would be lowered.

"Why are you here?" I finally asked.

He mulled over my question, as if digging for the answer that wouldn't turn me away. "I don't really know," he said.

Every week Preacher Man brought gifts of fudge that I admitted a craving for and writing tablets that I said I needed, but he never poked the embers from my past trying to kindle the answer to my future. He accepted me where I was. It was me who brought up Mama.

"I miss her."

"I imagine you do," he said.

My tight muscles began to relax each week as we walked the cobbled paths where hummingbirds fluttered around red bugle blooms. I scooped out small bites of myself and he gobbled them as if starved.

"Mama had gypsy blood," I said. "Her great–grandmother, Rosa, was queen of all the gypsies and people traveled miles for her to read their palms. When Mama danced, her arms and legs coiled like lassos."

Preacher Man pulled a small knife from his pocket, picked up a twig. The blade sparkled as it slid over knots and through rough bark. Still, I knew he swallowed every word I fed him.

"When I'd brush Mama's hair, I melted into it like I did into her songs." I trembled like I was fixing to fall apart, but I was too lost in memory. Preacher Man's hands became idle and he peered up at me. "I needed her," I said. "He took her away and I'll always hate him. Always."

"I understand." Preacher Man returned to the twig and knife in his hands.

On our way back to the cottage, I felt lighter, as if layers of me had been removed and left behind with Preacher Man's pile of wood shavings.

The cold hard winter was ending. We walked the path, hands in the pockets of our heavy coats, our breaths spurting out smoke.

"Do you know my daddy?"

"Yes."

I had figured that for a long time even though he'd never mentioned it. Above our silence were tweeting birds, chattering squirrels, and an airplane. The hyacinths were just breaking ground and forsythia bushes were yellow blooms. Dry winter grass crumpled beneath our feet. Oaks and maples were still naked. Strange how the beauty of life and ugliness of death lived together on the same hillside.

"How do you know him?"

"From prison."

The word *prison* struck me like the butt of that gun against Mama's skull. That day, I ran from Preacher Man, all the way back, up to my room, and into my bed.

I didn't see him again until the daisies were in full bloom. Warm breezes swept through the treetops and tall grasses, but still my bones felt brittle and frozen.

Preacher Man smiled when he saw me. We went on our walk as if our last meeting had been a fictional scene lost inside our realities.

"I brought you something," he said, "but I must confess." With this he stopped. "It's from your daddy." He must've read my disbelief because he started walking again. "I'll take it back to him."

"No." I still stood where we'd stopped. "What is it?" These last three words were a whisper.

From his shirt pocket, he passed me a picture and I climbed into it, into my mama's lap where I smelled vanilla in the cranny of her neck and felt the silkiness of her blouse across my cheek. My tears splattered on the picture and I wiped them from my and mama's images. The picture had been torn, my daddy's image cut away and I ran my finger over the tattered edge.

"He thought you'd want it that way."

"What does he know?" I shouted and I took off down the path, away from Preacher Man knowing he wouldn't try to stop me.

Winter trampled the land again and as powerful as the blazing sun was, it couldn't thaw the biting frost. Nothing conquered the coldness of death. Nothing.

For Christmas, I had given Preacher Man a mug that I made in a pottery class and he raved over it, saying how he had broken his favorite mug and how this would replace it. He handed over his present.

Tearing the package open, I froze seeing the hardback journal filled with gold–edged paper. My name, *Elizabeth Macy Goldwin* had been engraved on the cover.

"Like it?"

I stroked the elegant letters. "It's exactly what I would've chosen." I flipped through it, hearing the crispness of unused pages. "What're you hiding behind your back?"

The huge rectangular box behind him was anything but hidden.

"It's from your daddy."

I was tempted to run, to shut myself up in my room again, but it didn't seem right just receiving Preacher Man's gift.

"Hand it over." My hands shook. "It's freezing out here."

"You want to head back?"

"I'm fine. Really."

The silvery wrapping paper was covered in angels playing harps, flutes, and horns and I imagined Mama among them, dancing in the blue sea above. I slipped my fingers into the folds, trying not to tear the angels. The paper floated down, unveiling an intricately carved box, the size of a small trunk, its glossy finish as slick as glass.

"Made it himself," said Preacher Man.

Murdering hands created something so beautiful? I opened the heavy lid. Scents of fresh glazed wood and glue escaped and inside was lined in purple velvet.

I touched the envelope on bottom. "I'm scared."

"I know."

The envelope wasn't sealed, so I slid the card out. On front was, *Hope you have a Joyous Christmas and a Happy New Year.* On the inside, written in bad handwriting, was one word. *Daddy.*

"Didn't have much to say, did he?"

"Said you'd see through mushy words."

It was scary that my daddy still knew me, yet the realization almost calmed me. I tucked the card and the journal inside the chest.

Every time new emotions started sprouting up in me, I weeded myself with words in my journal. It was weird how those feelings sped down to my fingers and out onto the pages.

The letter arrived after New Year's Day, same handwriting on the same generic envelope. Out of habit, I ripped it in two before opening it. I dashed out to the bench, envelope halves in each hand, parts of me wrestling, tear it up, read it, tear it up, read it. The cold tore through my worn jeans and my house slippers. When I finally stopped crying, I pulled each half from the torn envelope, pieced them together.

I won't ever blame you for hating me. I am so very sorry. Daddy

I shredded the halves into confetti, which I tossed to the wind to sweep away. But his words blew back into my face, into my mind.

Spring came. I traveled with Preacher Man to Parchman, one minute saying, "I've made a mistake," the next saying, "No, I'm going." Preacher Man would've let me do whatever.

The secluded prison was in the middle of thousands of acres. Once inside, I emptied my pockets, followed a uniformed woman into the ladies room to be patted down like a criminal. Metal detectors couldn't detect the deadly weapon stashed inside of me. My own hatred.

Other people wore family reunion smiles and we all loaded the bus destined for my daddy's prison pod. Once there, a call to the back summoned my daddy to the visitor's room.

"I'm going to puke," I said.

"Bathroom's over there." Preacher Man pointed. "I'd offer to take you back, but the bus is gone."

"I'll be okay."

I flew into the restroom, fell against the door. At the sink, I splashed cold water on my face, dried it with stiff brown paper. Then I gazed into that dirty mirror. I leaned in closer to view two determined eyes staring back. I'd face this man who murdered my mama and cut him up into little pieces with the sharp blade of wrath.

Daddy walked through the doors. I saw him first. He wasn't at all like I had imagined, thin, weak, wasting away behind bars. No. He was strong, healthy, walked confidently. Preacher Man called out to him and he hurried toward him until his eyes met mine. He stopped. His eyes were different from the rest of him, too weak for his muscled body, afraid, and almost worn out. That was more like it.

He shook Preacher Man's hand, said, "How's it going, man?" He didn't reach out for me. "Lizzy. Good to see you."

It'd been a long time since I heard that name. "Elizabeth is her name," Mama had always reminded him, "like a queen. Not Lizzy, like a foolish girl with no sense."

"My name is Elizabeth."

His eyes darted to Preacher Man. I was in control now.

Outside, we sat at a picnic table where Preacher Man inquired about some kind of correspondence course Daddy was taking. I almost said something, surprised that my daddy was studying from a book, but I glared silently through the fence at other brick units behind wire fences, listening to Preacher Man and Daddy speak about prisoners they both knew, some who had gotten out and some who had just arrived.

"Anybody want a drink?" Preacher Man said.

I shook my head, but Daddy answered with, "An orange soda."

"One orange soda. Elizabeth, you sure? I'm buying."

I nodded. He left me to fidget on the wooden bench across from my daddy.

"Thanks for coming. I know this is hard." His words were like picks gouging my memory.

"You don't know shit." The pain grew intense in his eyes. "I hate you as much today as the day you murdered my mama."

He nodded.

Preacher Man arrived with cold drinks. My lips remained as tight as the last notch on my belt. My first visit went exactly as planned. I'd kill him off little by little.

Over the following months, my wrath continued torturing Daddy and he endured like a martyr. But my liberation never came. Instead, images seeped into my dreams, lies that had Mama embracing another man, giggling in his arms. I would wake up wide-eyed, trying to push those thoughts away.

On a Sunday, I sat across from Daddy at the picnic table. Preacher Man was talking to another inmate and his family.

"Why'd you tear the picture in half?" I asked.

"Picture?"

"The one of Mama and me. And you."

Daddy smiled, and when he did, I could see my laughing daddy from years ago. "Figured you'd want it that way," he said.

"You were right." He looked away. "So, why do you keep writing me? To save your lost soul?"

This time when his eyes met mine, they looked strong and sure. "No, Elizabeth. I keep writing because I found it."

His answer surprised me and I spun away, squeezing my eyes shut until they hurt. I didn't like what I saw, but I knew that what I saw was truth.

"Mama was with someone else," I whispered, testing the sound of that truth, expecting Daddy to reply with something like, "Told you so."

"I should've walked away, Lizzy. Let it be."

"If only—"

"You know what they say about hindsight, don't you?"

"It's twenty-twenty?"

"Nah. It ain't worth a damn."

"I miss her so much."

"So do I." Tears floated along his lids. He blinked, cutting them free. Several splattered the words *Jim was here, May 5, 1975* carved into the table.

I couldn't swallow my tears down. Flipping my legs over the bench, I raced to the bathroom, locked the door, and slumped down beside the toilet. Each time I thought I was finished crying, I'd wash my face, take deep breaths, but when I'd start to leave, I'd start up again.

It was a while before I returned to find Preacher Man beside my daddy, patting him. I plunked down across from them, silent, and drained.

The loudspeaker blasted, "Five minutes remaining for visitation."

Preacher Man stood. "You about ready?"

"In a minute." *Truth, truth* echoed in my brain. "Those things they said about Mama were true," I said.

Daddy held up his hand to stop my confession. "Enough, Lizzy. I have to live with what I did. Thing is, if your mama had left me for another man ..." He paused, as if gathering up all the letters to form his next words. "I would've still had my little girl."

His little girl.

"Two minutes," blared the loudspeaker

"Do you still have it?" I asked.

"What?"

"The other part of the picture."

"Yeah, but—"

"Get it."

Daddy bolted from the table, rushed into the building. Outside I paced, my legs heavy with impatience.

"One minute!"

I paced faster, head bowed, ignoring Preacher Man as he waited for me. "Come on, come on," I mumbled.

"Last call. Doors closing."

The door flung open and the officer stepped forward to push my daddy back into the building where they would lock him in. Daddy pleaded and the officer glanced back at me, his grimace softening into an understanding smile.

Daddy handed me the crinkled picture, frayed along one side and I carefully tucked it into my pocket. Before I had time to think, I rushed into my daddy's arms and we both cried as he stroked my hair.

"I'm sorry, Lizzy," he kept repeating, until the guard kindly nudged us apart.

That night, I removed the torn picture from the frame Preacher Man had given me, positioned Daddy's image next to Mama, and taped my family back together again.

Truth had released me from my prison. Mercy had released my daddy from his.

I removed the journal from the chest. The overhead light cast a glow on the glossy angel wrapping folded inside. I touched it, remembering the day I unveiled my daddy's plea. Grabbing a pen, I flipped on the lamp, and began to write.

Swee' Daddy's Big Sanyo
by Bob Strother

Marcie woke to the labored grinding of the trailer's single decade–old air conditioner unit. A hot Texas Panhandle sun had already set the windows ablaze and the inside air smelled of scorched metal and stale cigarette smoke. She rolled over and nestled against Swee' Daddy's neck, his loose blond curls tickling her nose. He'd let his hair grow out after some of the women at Dynamite Bill's and the Rock 'n Country had told him he favored Matthew McConaughey. He'd also read in People magazine that McConaughey never used deodorant, liking his "man-smell," and thereafter, Swee' Daddy showered only every other day. Marcie didn't mind much, as long as he didn't carry it too far and bathed before they made love.

Swee' Daddy stirred and shifted over onto his back. "Gotta get going. Arliss'll be here in 'bout fifteen minutes."

He popped out of bed and padded down the hall to the trailer's tiny bathroom. Marcie got out of the bed and slipped into a chenille robe. "You want some breakfast, Swee' Daddy?" she asked, heading into the kitchen area.

The mattress springs creaked as he sat fitting his jeans over the tops of his lizard-skin boots, and then he appeared in the kitchen entranceway buttoning a pale-blue yoked shirt. "Just coffee, I guess. We'll get something on the road."

Arliss arrived ten minutes later, punctual as usual, and beeped the horn of the company truck. Marcie walked to the door and waved to Arliss, who grinned at her and waved back. Swee' Daddy came up alongside her, squaring a cream-colored Stetson on his head.

"Be good," she told him.

"Sweetheart, you know I will." He winked and slipped his arms around her, cupping her buttocks in his hands and squeezing.

She glanced toward the truck, color rising in her cheeks, but Arliss sat staring straight ahead like a department-store mannequin. Then Swee' Daddy's tongue slid between her lips and she forgot all about Arliss.

* * *

I'm a lucky girl, Marcie thought, watching the North Texas Communications truck trailing a plume of dust toward the flat horizon. Who'd have figured she–in all her God-given mediocrity–would end up roping the most eligible maverick in Dallam County. Not that he was perfect, but what man was? A couple of recent DWI arrests had Swee' Daddy's driver's license residing at the Texas Department of Public Safety for an as-yet-undetermined period. In the interim, he'd drafted his co-worker, Arliss, as his all-around designated driver. That was part of the man's natural charm–that ability to engender easy favor from men and women alike. What he'd seen in her she wasn't sure, but she had decided not to dwell on it. "Don't look a gift horse in the mouth," her mother told her years ago. Well, she wasn't about to look askance at this stallion.

He was back on Friday, and they spent the weekend making love and watching DVDs on the new television. Two months before, on the evening after he'd moved into the trailer, she'd found him standing in the living area, arms crossed over his chest, studying the little seventeen–inch Toshiba she'd had since she graduated high school. "We're gonna have to do something about that little pissant TV," he'd said.

The next day, they'd taken her truck to the Wal–Mart in Dalhart, and he'd paid nearly four hundred dollars for a new twenty–eight–inch Sanyo. She'd been thrilled, not with the TV itself, but because it seemed like such a "couple" kind of thing to do. She'd made a meatloaf that night to celebrate, and later they'd lain naked and entwined on the sofa, flickering images from the television reflecting softly off their sweat–drenched skin.

"Me and Arliss have to go do some line work up near the Oklahoma border this week," he told her on Monday. "Probably won't be back 'til late Wednesday, but I'll call every day." They had breakfast together, then she kissed him goodbye and waved to Arliss, and sent them on their way. After work that evening and again on Tuesday, she made up tuna casseroles–Swee' Daddy's favorite–and put them in the freezer for when he returned. They talked on the phone at night, and he told her he missed her and that Arliss couldn't play poker for shit. Swee' Daddy was already up eighteen dollars, and if his luck held out, he'd take her for a movie and ice cream on Saturday night.

Marcie got worried when she hadn't seen or heard from Swee' Daddy by midnight on Wednesday. She was still awake, drinking coffee and biting her fingernails when she heard tires crunching on gravel two hours later. Arliss was out of the truck by the time she got to the door. "Where's Swee' Daddy?" she asked, hurrying barefooted down the concrete blocks that served as her front steps.

Arliss moved around to the passenger side of the truck and opened the door. "He's here ... and he's fine, I reckon, depending on your perspective." He leaned in and grabbed Swee' Daddy by the arms and wrestled him around to where his feet were hanging out of the truck cab. Then he bent and hefted the other man over his shoulder into a fireman's carry, and walked over to Marcie. "He's not hurt or nothing, just drunk. Uh ... where you want him? In the bed?"

Marcie nodded and followed Arliss back into the trailer. When Swee' Daddy was laid out unconscious on the bed, she asked, "What happened?"

Arliss stood with his hands on his hips, not looking at her. "I'd rather not get involved, Marcie. He can tell you after he wakes up, I guess, if he wants to."

Marcie's face went hot, and she felt her pulse throbbing at her temples. "Don't you tell me that, Arliss Shaw. You were with him. You were part and parcel to whatever went on, and you owe me some kind of explanation. I've been worried sick."

Arliss turned and faced her and his features softened, and she was sure she saw something resembling pity in his eyes.

"Actually," he said, "I wasn't with him. I left him at Dynamite Bill's sometime around nine o'clock. He said he'd get a ride home after he'd had a couple of drinks."

That left Marcie confused. "But you're with him now. What—"

"I got a call," Arliss said, "to come get him."

"They called from the bar? Why didn't Bill call me to come for him? Lord knows, he's driven me home a couple of times when I've had too much."

Arliss stuffed his hands into his pockets, walked into the living area, and stood looking out the front–door window. After a moment, he said, "It wasn't the bar called, Marcie."

"Then who?"

"It was Alma Forester."

Marcie's knees went weak. "Alma Forester?" She backed up until she felt the edge of the sofa behind her, and then sank down onto it.

"I've got to go," Arliss said. "I'm sorry for your trouble."

Marcie heard the truck start up and pull away. She sat, hugging herself and trembling even though she was fully dressed and the trailer was still warm from the afternoon heat. After a while, she got up and went into the bedroom and stood looking down at Swee' Daddy, who was lying on his back, snoring softly. The crotch of his jeans was still dark where he had pissed himself at some point. *Probably in Alma Forester's bed*, she thought. *Otherwise that slut wouldn't have bothered calling Arliss.*

She tugged off his jeans and underwear, trying to ignore the lipstick residue on Swee' Daddy's stomach and the elastic band of his briefs, and stuffed them into a big black trash bag. Then she opened the closet and chest of drawers and added the rest of his clothes, including the white shirt with pearl stud snaps she'd pressed so carefully earlier in the evening. "Liar," she said. "Bastard."

It had been three days since Marcie kicked Swee' Daddy out, him first denying everything, then pleading for her forgiveness, and finally dragging his clothes behind him out to the road. She'd been resolute in her anger, but now suffered its empty aftermath. She'd tried watching television, just for the noise, but it didn't help. She'd had her hair done after work, paying forty dollars for a new cut and blonde highlights, but that hadn't helped either. She picked at her food, and then dumped it into the garbage. She thought about going to one of the two bars in Dalhart, but she was afraid she'd run into Swee' Daddy or, worse, Alma Forester. She was sitting on the sofa, staring at the walls, when there was a knock on her door.

"Marcie?" It was Swee' Daddy.

She went to the door and looked out. He was standing at the bottom of the steps, an unfamiliar Chevrolet sedan parked in the gravel drive.

"What the hell do you want?" she asked.

"Open the door," he said. "I just want to talk."

She opened the door. The Chevy's engine was ticking as it cooled, and a gentle breeze filled the air with tiny cottonwood tufts from the trees behind the trailer. "Whose car is that?"

Swee' Daddy turned and looked at it for a moment as though he had been unaware of the Chevy's existence. Then he shrugged and said, "It belongs to Alma."

"You get your license back?"

He ignored the question. Instead, he said, "I've come to get the TV."

"We bought it together," she said.

"Yeah, well I paid for it, so it's mine."

"You lived with me two months rent–free. I figure the TV's half mine."

Swee' Daddy shook his head and spat into the dust, sliding his hands down into the back pockets of his jeans. "Now, look, Marcie–"

"Damn you, cheater!" She slammed the door so hard the glasses rattled above the sink.

Three days later, Marcie came home to find a note taped to the front door of the trailer: Marcie–not Dear Marcie, she noted, just Marcie. If you don't give me back the Sanyo–for which I have a duplicate bill of sale that I got from Ron's TV and Appliances yesterday–I will sue you for it in small claims court. It was signed Leonard, which was Swee' Daddy's given name, and the "I will sue you" part was underlined.

Marcie called him at work the following morning. "You can have the damned Sanyo, but I don't want you inside the trailer again. I'll meet you in the parking lot at the American Legion baseball field after work."

It was all she could do to get the TV out of the trailer and into the bed of her Ford camper truck, but she managed on a hefty combination of white–hot anger and sheer determination. On her lunch break, she grabbed a quick burger at the Dairy Queen, stopped off at Dewey's Pawn Palace, and made it back to work with five minutes to spare.

Four hours later, she sat on the folded down tailgate of the pickup, the Sanyo beside her, its big blank screen a replica of the empty feeling she had deep in the pit of her stomach. The North Texas Communications truck pulled into the lot at ten after five and parked twenty yards from the Ford. Arliss and Swee' Daddy climbed out of the truck, and Arliss tipped his hat to her and leaned back against the front fender.

Swee' Daddy adjusted his Stetson and swaggered over, a barely concealed smirk showing on his handsome face. "I'm glad you saw the light about this, Marcie. No hard feelings, huh?" The smirk changed to a self-satisfied smile.

Marcie shook her head. "No hard feelings," she said, "Leonard."

His smile faded. "I can't help what my parents named me. Nobody can." He studied her for a moment, letting his eyes roam over her face and body. "Maybe your parents should have named you Mousey instead of Marcie. It would've fit your looks and personality better." He slid the television to the edge of the tailgate, grabbed it by the bottom, and began walking back to the company truck.

Marcie whipped Dewey's little Saturday Night Special from the back waistband of her jeans, thrust it out in front of her, and squeezed the trigger. Swee' Daddy yelped like a mongrel dog as the .22 caliber round tore into his left calf, and then he and the Sanyo tumbled forward onto the ground.

A small trickle of gray smoke wafted back into Marcie's face and the acrid odor of cordite filled her nostrils. It hadn't been quite like what she'd expected. There was no spray of blood like there was in the movies they'd watched on the big TV, just a little dark spot where the bullet punctured the denim of Swee' Daddy's jeans.

Arliss jumped like he was the one shot when the gun went off, then stood staring at Marcie open-mouthed as

Swee' Daddy flopped and flailed about like a fish on the riverbank.

"Goddamn, Marcie!" Arliss said.

She met his gaze and the two regarded each other–thoughtfully, it seemed to her–for a long moment.

On the ground between them, Swee' Daddy hugged his left leg, alternately cursing Marcie and mewling like a kitten. "Goddamn it, Arliss, don't just stand there! Come help get me away from this bitch before she shoots me again."

"Goddamn, Marcie," Arliss said again.

She tilted her head a little to one side and smiled. Before Arliss tore his gaze away from her and started over to where Swee' Daddy lay, she was pretty sure he was smiling, too.

Arliss helped Swee' Daddy into the truck, then came over and stood in front of Marcie and took off his hat. "I don't think there'll be much to that wound, Marcie. It looks like the bullet just nicked the side of the calf. I'll get it cleaned up and bandaged. He might favor that leg for a few days, but he'll be all right."

Marcie licked her lips and looked up into Arliss's face, squinting into the late afternoon sun. "You think he might send the sheriff after me?"

Arliss glanced back at the truck. "I kind of doubt it. He's not too keen on being around the jailhouse. I'll talk to him if I need to, but if I was you, I wouldn't worry about it."

He turned to go but paused beside the Sanyo still lying in the tall grass alongside the third baseline. Setting it back upright, he brushed debris from the speaker slots and used his shirtsleeve to clean the screen, which appeared intact in spite of the fall. "I'll come back for the television after I get him taken care of."

Marcie nodded, and then watched as the truck disappeared in the distance. After a bit, she slid down off the tailgate and strolled over toward the TV, stopping about ten feet in front of it. She squatted on her haunches, took careful aim, and squeezed the trigger again. The revolver's report was sharp in the still Texas air, and a small round hole appeared in the center of the dark screen. Vein–like cracks fissured out from the hole's diameter like a spider's web. *Dead solid perfect,* she thought.

Walking back to the pickup, Marcie's steps trailed miniature puffs of ochre–colored dust. The sun was warm on her shoulders, and she picked up a sweet fragrance from the Tea Olives lining the outer lengths of the baseball field.

She thought about the funny way Arliss had smiled when Swee' Daddy had gone down. Thought she might invite him over for a tuna casserole sometime.

J. B. and the Jug
by Ovid Vickers

That Wednesday morning when Mr. McDaniel, our mail carrier, delivered the Telfair County Times, I opened the paper and read the death notices. Well, right there on the same page with those who had gone on to a greater glory was this ad from the Citizens Bank announcing that a gallon thermos jug would be given away to any person opening a new savings account of fifty dollars or more.

Soon as I finished reading the ad, I went looking for J. B. He was in the side yard changing the air filter in the pickup. So I waited until he finished with the air filter, and then I said, "You reckon there's fifty dollars in that syrup bucket you keep under the bed?"

You see, J. B. has kept a syrup bucket under the bed ever since we got married, and if he has some loose change, he just pitches it in the bucket. Well, he assured me there was well over fifty dollars under the bed. Then he said, "What are you up to?"

And then I said, "Listen, it's as much my money as it is yours, and I read this ad in the paper saying the Citizens Bank will give a thermos jug to anybody who opens a savings account.

"I'm not changing banks for a thermos jug," J. B. said. "We have always kept our money down at the Planters Bank where Cousin Will Henry Johnson is in charge of accounts."

As J. B. let down the pickup hood, he said, "Cousin Will Henry is a deacon and on top of that he is also a Gideon. Listen to this; when I was a little boy and he gave his testimony on Gideon Sunday and told how that Gideon Bible in his jacket pocket slowed down a German bullet and kept it from piercing his heart, I decided right then and there that when I got grown I was going to put my money in that bank for him to look after.

"And besides," J. B. continued, "Ruby Lee Rodgers works in the Citizens Bank, and when she went to work there you told me that just because I had taken her to some high school parties the summer before she went off to business school, you'd keep our money in an old mayonnaise jar before you'd deposit it anywhere she worked."

I looked at J.B. and said, "Listen, we need a thermos jug, and I'm not the one going in the bank. You're going to take the bucket of money and get them to run it through that new coin separator, and bring me home a thermos jug."

When Saturday came, J. B. took the money to the Citizens Bank, and of course, I expected him to come home with the thermos. But No! He deposited the money all right, but he didn't bring home any thermos. He said Ruby Lee told him they had run out and didn't have a single thermos left. He declared that he got to talking to her and before he knew it, she had already filled out the receipt for his bucket of money.

Well, you can imagine how this made me feel. The more I thought about it, the madder I got. I decided right then and there I was going to have that thermos come hell or high water!

"J.B.," I said, "we're going to town just as soon as you finish getting that hay out of the lower bottom." J. B. didn't much want to go, but I knew my rights. The paper said I would get a thermos jug, and I was bound and determined that if the bank kept my money, I was going to have a thermos.

Well, it was the next Wednesday before we finally got to town, and as J. B. parked the truck in front of the bank I could see Ruby Lee through the big plate glass window. Just as we went through the front door, she gathered up some papers and went back toward the vault. So I just stepped right up to one of the teller windows and said, "I'd like to have a word with Ruby Lee Rodgers, please."

One of the girls went to get her, and even though it was banking hours, she came out of the vault running a comb, right nonchalant like, through her moussed hair. I don't do anything to my hair. I never tease it, and I'm sure not going to mousse it. But Ruby Lee had moussed hers and then fluffed it out. She might think it's pretty, but the way it stands out around her face, it looks just like she exploded two or three fire crackers in it.

She stopped running that long-toothed comb through her hair when I said, "Ruby Lee, didn't that ad in the paper say that every customer opening a new account would get a gallon thermos?"

With that, Ruby Lee kinda dropped her eyelids and mumbled, "Well, yes."

I said, "Well, I've come to get mine."

Then she said, "I'm sorry, but we ran out right before J. B. came in here last Wednesday."

"All right," I said, "In that case, I'll withdraw."

She looked over at Bessie Graham at the window next to her and said, "Did you tell me we had a few more of those thermos jugs down in the basement?"

"Yes," Bessie replied, "but Mr. Hightower is out of the office and there isn't anyone to go down there for one."

"Never mind," I said. "J.B. will be glad to go down into the basement with Ruby Lee."

They looked at one another kinda sheepish like. Then Ruby Lee came from behind her window and opened a door in the lobby that led to a basement staircase. I waited at the top of the stairs. When they were about halfway down, Ruby Lee tripped and fell. She tried to make it look like an accident, but I could tell she did it on purpose.

I knew she expected J.B. to put his arm around her to keep her from falling, but I was standing right there and J.B. didn't reach for her at all. The next thing I knew, Ruby Lee was all sprawled out at the bottom of the stairs, with J.B. standing over her.

She hollered and carried on like she didn't have any raising at all, and J.B. looked up at me and called, "Ruby Lee fell, and I'm bringing her back up."

"Not without my thermos jug," I called back down.

So, after J.B. put the thermos handle over his right arm, he picked Ruby Lee up in both arms. As he was bringing her up the stairs, I decided she wasn't hurt half as much as she was pretending to be. The thing that really got me was that I could see she had put one of her arms around J.B.'s shoulder in a tight squeeze. I watched as they came up the stairs, and believe me I was mad!

J.B. brought her into the lobby, and when he went to put her down on the couch, she sorta clung to him a little longer than I thought was necessary for her safety.

They called Dr. Ledlow, and he said she had really sprained her ankle. Well, even if she did sprain her ankle, it served her right. She had lied about that thermos jug. She had pretended to fall just to get J.B. to pay her some attention, and she had clung to my husband like a leech while he was trying to help her in her misery.

After Dr. Ledlow got her ankle wrapped, we started home. But before we left town, I asked J.B. to stop by the paper office so I could get a copy of the latest Telfair County Times. When I opened that paper, my heart just fell. Right there was an ad which said, "Add fifty dollars to your savings account at the Planters Bank, and we will give you a new electric coffee pot absolutely free."

You know we need a new coffee pot a lot worse than we ever needed a thermos jug.

The Break In
by Glanda Widger

It was three a.m. when Lorelei's eyes popped open. She had heard a faint sound coming from the front of the house. She held her breath and listened. There it was again. There was nothing else to do except go and investigate. She slipped quietly down the dark hallway, the small twenty–two pistol held at her side. *Heck,* she thought to herself, *I should have gotten the thirty–eight like the salesman suggested.* At the time the other gun had felt too heavy and bulky, like carrying a brick in her purse. "A bit much for a southern lady of indeterminate age," she had murmured.

The noises were barely audible. Nevertheless she knew someone was in her house. There was nothing for it but to use the little popgun. She knew that the bullet would not kill the intruder. Hopefully, it would at least slow him down some so she could call the police. Her marksmanship was a little rusty, though she still remembered how from when Daddy taught her the fine art of shooting.

Slipping around the doorway that led to the living room, she could just make out the form of a man rummaging through the old china hutch. *Well, at least he was discriminating. A younger man would have gone directly for the electronics.* She straightened up and pointed the gun.

"Excuse me Darlin'," she said, in her soft southern drawl, "But I think ya'll have the wrong house. Now why don't you just run along before you get me any more upset." Reaching out with her other hand, she flipped on the light.

The middle-aged man stood up...and up...and up. Judging from his size, Lorelei now wished she had purchased a bazooka. Determinedly, she held the little pistol steady. He eyed the small gun and smiled, displaying several rotten teeth. "Well now, old lady, why don't you just run on back to your bedroom and let me get on with my business? You ain't gonna do no damage with that toy. If you behave, then we'll manage just fine."

Lorelei had to pretty much agree. Shooting this mountain of a man with the gun she held was tantamount to shooting a gorilla with a BB gun. It would really tick him off, but not do any great damage. Still, she would not just meekly obey his orders. And she took offense at being called an "old lady." She was still in her prime, after all.

"Well Honey, I just can't let you steal my granny's silver, now can I? I'm afraid I'll just have to shoot you and take my chances. I reckon enough bullets will stop even someone as big as you." *Why in God's name am I carrying on a conversation with a thief?* She wondered.

"Naw. I know you ain't gonna pull that trigger. I bet that thing ain't even loaded. Now, be a good girl and I won't have to hurt you. I hate hurting little old ladies, but a man has to do what a man has to do."

The gun never wavered. "I assure you sir, this gun is loaded, and I will shoot you if you do not leave immediately. Please be so kind as to go out the way you came in."

Lorelei was getting tired of this silly conversation, and, she was getting mad. The burglar did not realize what a bad idea it was to upset her. He took a step forward. She raised her arm, took careful aim, and shot him in the kneecap, just like her daddy had shown her.

The man/mountain screamed as he fell over her antique end table. Not only that, he also broke her mama's antique lamp, the one with the little cherubs on it. After a few seconds of blistering profanities, he levered himself up on his one good leg. "I ain't playing no more," he gasped. "You little witch! Why couldn't you just leave well enough alone? Now I gotta hurt you real bad. An' I just hate doing things like that."

Lorelei calmly took aim again and blew a small hole in the other kneecap. This time her burglar did not get up. He rudely lay there bleeding all over her nice carpet and screeching like some silly old woman. *There just weren't any manly men around anymore,* she mused.

"Darn it, now look what you've done," she complained as she dialed 911. "You just ruined a perfectly good carpet. Now quiet down, I can't hear the operator. Hello, Laura Jean, this is Lorelei Buckner at 20 Woodhaven Road. I need to report a burglary. The screaming? Oh, that's the burglar. No, he's okay, I only shot him twice. Thank you, I'll be waiting for them."

It was after daybreak before everyone was finally gone from the little house. Lorelei had made a pot of coffee and brought out the cookies she had baked last evening. She insisted the poor paramedics have refreshments before taking the groaning man away. It was not their fault that they had to be called out of their warm beds so early.

The sheriff stayed behind and chatted while finishing off the last of the cookies. At last, he stood, dusted the crumbs from his uniform and bid her have a good day.

Lorelei waved to him from her front door. "Bye Amos and thank you for everything. I sure am sorry about waking everyone up on a Saturday morning. You tell those darlin' boys from the ambulance to just stop by anytime."

She walked into the living room and began to tidy up. She was going to be very upset if the blood left a spot in her lovely Persian rug. Sighing she realized that she was going to have to go back to the gun shop. The twenty–two was just not an adequate weapon for a poor helpless woman who lived alone.

Author Notes

Allgood, Marlyn, at 76, divides her time between her homes in Michigan and Mississippi. In her retirement, she has found time to fulfill a lifelong ambition to write. She is a member of the Gulf Coast Writers Association and the Mississippi Writers Guild. Her work has appeared in several regional journals and magazines including *DeSoto Magazine* and the *Oxford So and So*. She and her husband Fred have enjoyed the contrasts between the climate, the language and the customs of Mississippi and Michigan.

Bardwell, Shannon Rulè enjoys non-fiction writing including memoir, humor, devotional, newspaper features and short stories. Her fiction stories are "fiction" but every word of them is practically true. She is published in numerous anthologies and has won several writing awards the latest being for *God Bless the Boon* awarded by the Delta Writer's Association's Tennessee Williams Literary Festival. Bardwell was born in the South, raised in the Delta, lived abroad, and later returned to her native land where she claims, "There is no place like home."

Beamguard, Betty Wilson writes magazine features, short fiction, poetry and humorous essays. She has received over thirty honors for her writing. Her work has appeared in *Women in the Outdoors, South Carolina, Sasee, ByLine, The Writer* and more. Two dozen of her short stories have been published or accepted. Betty has also written the biography of a woman who drives a draft horse with her feet—*How Many Angels Does It Take: The Remarkable Life of Heather Rose Brooks*.
www.home.earthlink.net/~bbeamguard

Boggan, Lottie is a resident of Jackson, Mississippi, a long time Contributing Writer for the *Northside Sun Newspaper*, and in 2007 won the first prize in the state for my column. She won First Place in the Division of Novels in the Eudora Welty Film and Festival, and has won numerous other awards. With Judy Tucker, she published three anthologies of short stories of Mississippi authors, *From the Sleeping Porch, Fireflies in Fruit Jars*, and *Mad Dogs and Moonshine.*

Budavari, Susan has written two psychological suspense novels, several award-winning short stories and co–edited and contributed to three mystery anthologies, the most recent, *Medium of Murder* (Red Coyote Press, 2008). Prior to that, she worked in chemical research and scientific information management in the pharmaceutical industry and was Editor of *The Merck Index*, a best–selling encyclopedia of chemicals, drugs and biologicals. She is an avid portrait painter and photographer of the desert landscape in Arizona, where she and her husband reside.

Chubbuck, Linda. Born in Chicago, grew up in Florida, lived in Alaska, and she now lives in a cottage on the cliffs of Ireland overlooking the Atlantic Ocean. Her interests vary from scuba diving in the Keys to spelunking Kentucky caves, salmon fishing, gold mining at Resurrection Creek, Alaska and lately, writing. She's published three short stories and hopes to expand that number. Being Irish, she often uses Celtic folklore in her themes, but loves the southern America experience and culture.

Davis, Ed. West Virginia native Ed Davis is a writing teacher at Sinclair Community College in Dayton, Ohio as well as the author of four poetry chapbooks, including *Healing Arts* (Pudding House, 2005); the novels *I Was So Much Older Then* (Disc-Us Books, 2001) and *The Measure of Everything* (Plain View Press, 2005). His story *"Power in the Blood"* will appear in Dots on a Map (Main Street Rag Press) in May, 2009. Please visit him at www.davised.com.

Dixon, Lucy J. holds a Masters of Library Information Science and is a librarian (she likes the old pedigree) at an elementary school in Gulfport, MS. She has received several awards for her writing, shaped, she says, by her experiences growing up in historic Natchez, MS. The proud mother of three sons, Lucy enjoys painting, gardening, reading, and of course, writing. *A woman must have money and a room of her own if she is to write fiction.* Virginia Woolf

Farris, Fred a retired Kansas City advertising agency president, now writes short fiction for fun. His stories have won national awards for prose in *ByLine Magazine* and his story, *"Cello Bells"* is scheduled to be released in fall, 2009 in *Goose River Anthology*. His short fiction has been published in *Kansas City Voices Magazine,* and *Best Times Magazine.* Farris is a member of The Kansas City Writers' Group. He lives in Leawood,, KS. Visit him at ffarris1@kc.rr.com

Floyd, John has more than 800 publishing credits in magazines like *The Strand, Writer's Digest, Woman's World, Alfred Hitchcock's Mystery Magazine,* and *Ellery Queen's Mystery Magazine.* A 2007 Derringer Award winner, John is the author of two collections of short fiction: *Rainbow's End* (2006) and *Midnight* (2008).

Gable, Brenda is a native of the Carolinas. Born in Wilmington, NC she was a natural beach bum; fishing, seashell hunting, and swimming at coastal beaches. She turned her skills to fiction after writing professionally for the government for over twenty years. Brenda loves all things in nature and is an avid horsewoman and gardener. She lives with her husband, five cats, and a horse in Pelion, SC. Her prior publication is *The Pirate of Buzzard Bay*.

Gates, Nancy Gotter lives in High Point, North Carolina with her cat Annie. She's had thirty short stories published in various anthologies and literary magazines as well as four mysteries, one set in Sarasota, Florida and the rest in Greensboro, NC. When she isn't writing, she loves to paint, especially children. She has a mainstream novel, *Sand Castles*, coming out in November which is also set in Sarasota.

Hartman, Edward is a retired educator. He taught computer Science and mathematics at Purdue University and West Virginia University. He also taught English and mathematics at various high schools. He lives on a farm in southern West Virginia with wife Peggy and two sons. He began writing poetry in 1963, and has a book of poetry published this year (2009). He has also written a number of short stories and is polishing two fantasy novels, which he hopes to published this year.

Hearne, Dixon is the author of a new book, *Plantatia: Hightone and Lowdown Stories of the South* (Southeast Missouri University Press 2009). He is one of fifty authors selected to appear in *Woodstock Revisited: 50 Far Out, Groovy, Peace-Loving, Flashback-Inducing Stories From Those Who Were There* (Adams Media, June 2009). Also forthcoming is work in *Christmas Traditions* (Adams Media, September 2009). His stories, essays and poems appear widely in magazines and journals. The author can be reached at: www.dixonhearne.com and dixonh@socal.rr.com

Ledford, Deb. Three time nominee for the Pushcart Prize, Deborah's award-winning short stories appear in the print publications: *Arizona Literary Magazine, Forge Journal literary magazine, Twisted Dreams Magazine, AnthologyBuilder, Sniplits* and two Red Coyote Press mystery anthologies. A flash fiction piece is presented via podcast at *Sniplits.* Her psychological suspense thriller *Staccato* will be published by Second Wind Publishing, fall, 2009. Visit Deborah's website at: www.deborahjledford.com

Levin, Philip L. President of the GCWA (producers of this anthology), editor of their magazine *Magnolia Quarterly,* co-editor of this anthology, and coordinator of the "Let's Write" contest, Philip encourages hundreds of writers. Relaxing at his desk, enjoying the view of the Gulf waters, Philip contemplates the often asked, "Where do you get inspiration?" With a satisfying medical profession, a joyful writing hobby, and three wonderful children, he lives his stories. After all, isn't fiction actually autobiographical?

Loving, Denton lives on a farm near the historic Cumberland Gap, where Tennessee, Kentucky and Virginia come together. He works at Lincoln Memorial University, where he co-directs the Mountain Heritage Literary Festival. His story *Authentically Weathered Lumber* received the 2007 Gurney Norman Prize through the journal Kudzu. His story *A Sorrow of Mothers* won the 2008 Alabama Writers Conclave Fiction Prize. Other work has appeared in *Birmingham Arts Journal, Appalachian Journal, Somnambulist Quarterly, Heartland Review* and in numerous anthologies.

Lynch, Sylvia has published two nonfiction books. *Aristocracy's Outlaw* is a biography of "Doc" Holliday and *Harvey Logan in Knoxville* is about a member of Butch Cassidy's Wild Bunch. Her short fiction has appeared in the *Louisville Review, Kudzu*, anthologies *Motif: Writing by Ear*, and *We All Live Downstream*. She was the recipient of the 2008 Gurney Norman Prize for Fiction and placed first in the 2008 Tennessee Mountain Writers nonfiction competition. Lynch lives in East Tennessee.

McCann, M. L., award winning author, is best known for her *Longjohners' Mystery Series* for young adults, a literacy project to which she's devoted the past six years. Born in the Yukon, raised in Seattle, she has traveled the United States and Europe with her husband pursuing their Arabian horse business. Before settling down to write serious fiction, McCann worked as a scenic photographer. She lives with her husband in Scottsdale, Arizona.

McKee, Annie B. *Bluebirds and Buzzards* tells the hilarious undercurrents of a Mississippi beauty pageant. Annie is listed on the Mississippi Artist Roster, sponsored by Mississippi Arts Commission, as a Literary and Performing Artist. She is active with the arts and educational communities throughout Mississippi as storyteller, writer, newspaper columnist, playwright, creator of historic literary events, and Mississippi heritage projects. Her next book *Historic Photos of Mississippi* will publish May 2009.

Miles, Terry I. lives on the Mississippi Gulf Coast and is a 1997 graduate of Jefferson Davis Junior College and a 1999 alumni of the University of Southern Mississippi with a BA in English and History. Her creative writing talents have garnered her numerous awards in poetry, short stories and nine Cozy Little Murder Mysteries which she began in 2004. Since then she has also published two children's books. Be looking for her tenth murder mystery this fall and her eleventh one in the Spring of 2010.

Newman, Jan Rider has published fiction, poetry, and nonfiction in several literary journals. This is her first anthology. She wrote *Goose Chase* based on childhood memories of growing up in the middle of some rice fields along with several other families who where sharecroppers for the same landowner. One time a couple of the other men got into trouble after an illegal nighttime goose hunt. Emmy's part of the story developed from the unfulfilled ambitions of someone close to me.

Putnam, Richelle has been published in print and online publications in both adult and children's literature, including *The Copperfield Review*, *Cup of Comfort* inspirational books, *The Institute of Children's Literature*, *Boy's Quest*, *Appleseeds*, and *Hopscotch Magazine*, and many anthologies. As a writing instructor, she received formal education in creative writing from The Open College for the Arts, Writers Digest, The Institute of Children's Literature, and New York's Gotham Writers. She is listed on the Artist Roster for the State of Mississippi.

Strother, Bob, a recent Pushcart Prize nominee, has written creatively for just over five years, and has over three dozen publishing credits. He has written three novels, one of which has been published, and is currently working on a fourth. He took top honors in fiction and poetry in the 2008 issue of *The Petigru Review*, and has received other awards from the Green River (Kentucky) Writers' Association and the Carrie McCray Memorial Literary Awards program. Bob's website is: www.bobstrother.net

Vickers, Ovid received his B.A., M.A. and Ed.S. degrees from George Peabody College of Vanderbilt University. After serving in the military during the Korean Conflict, he began teaching English at East Central Community College in Decatur, Mississippi, where he served for more than 40 years. His short stories, articles, and poems have appeared in numerous publications, including *Texas Review, Delta Scene, Southern Living, Mississippi Magazine*, and *Mississippi Folklore Register*. For many years, he has written a weekly column for several local newspapers.

Widger, Glanda is a freelance humorist and a granny from the foothills of North Carolina. She writes for fun and poverty. For her, writing about the funny side of life is an addiction. She is a member of Writers with Humor (WWH)—everybody in the group knows that writing is her way of staving off running barefoot through cow pastures. She has been published in one other anthology and has garnered a few honorable mentions in various writing contests.